PENGUIN BOOKS

SHAKUNTALA

Namita Gokhale is an award winning writer and festival director. She is the author of eleven works of fiction and has written extensively on myth as well as the Himalayan region. Her acclaimed debut novel, *Paro: Dreams of Passion*, was published in 1984. Her recent novel, *Jaipur Journals*, published in January 2020, was set against the backdrop of the vibrant Jaipur Literature Festival. *Betrayed By Hope*, a play on the life of Michael Madhusudan Dutt, was also published in 2020.

A co-founder and co-director of the Jaipur Literature Festival, Gokhale is committed to supporting translations and curating literary dialogues across languages and cultures. She was conferred the Centenary National Award for Literature by the Assam Sahitya Sabha in Guwahati in 2017. She won the Sushila Devi Literature Award for her novel *Things to Leave Behind*, which also received the Best Fiction Jury Award at the Valley of Words Literature Festival 2017 and was on the longlist for the 2018 International Dublin Literary Award. She was also conferred the Sahitya Akademi (National Academy of Letters) Award for 2021 for her novel *Things To Leave Behind*.

T0290375

PRAISE FOR SHAKUNTALA

'Namita Gokhale writes grippingly about death, love and lust.'
—Khushwant Singh

'[Gokhale's] Shakuntala is a female counterpart of Hesse's Siddhartha, a seeker who must follow the trail of her destiny without looking back . . . Gokhale is drunk with the sound of words and that itself makes for a hypnotic read . . . This is Shakuntala for the 21st century.'—*India Today*

'An intriguing interplay of history and myth, suffused with profound metaphysical queries about the self . . . Gokhale's gripping and nuanced narrative offers a colourful template of ancient Indian life . . . [her] style is richly sensuous.'—*The Telegraph*

'One can almost feel the heat of the burning pyres on the ghats of Benares . . . The rhythm of life along the Ganges poignantly comes to life.'—*The Pioneer*

SHAKUNTALA

~ THE PLAY OF MEMORY ~

NAMITA GOKHALE

PENGUIN BOOKS

An imprint of Penguin Random House

PENGUIN BOOKS

USA | Canada | UK | Ireland | Australia
New Zealand | India | South Africa | China

Penguin Books is part of the Penguin Random House group of companies
whose addresses can be found at global.penguinrandomhouse.com

Published by Penguin Random House India Pvt. Ltd
4th Floor, Capital Tower 1, MG Road,
Gurugram 122 002, Haryana, India

First published in Viking by Penguin Books India 2005
This edition published in Penguin Books by Penguin Random House India in 2023

Copyright © Namita Gokhale 2005

ISBN 9780143062271

For sale in the Indian Subcontinent only

Typeset in *Perpetua* by SÜRYA, New Delhi
Printed at Gopsons Papers Pvt. Ltd., Noida.

www.penguin.co.in

Benares is a city of no mean antiquity. Twenty-five centuries ago, at the least, it was famous. When Babylon was struggling with Nineveh for supremacy . . . when Athens was growing in strength, before Rome had become known . . . she had already risen to greatness . . . While many cities and nations have fallen into decay and perished, her sun has never gone down; on the contrary, for long ages past it has shone with almost meridian splendour.

—Benares: The Sacred City of the Hindus
Rev. M.A. Sherring, 1868

शकुन्तला—(आत्मगतम् ।) हिअअ, पढमं एव्व सुद्धोवणदे मणोरहे कादरभावं ण मुञसि । साणुसअविद्धिअस्स मह दे संफद संदाबो । (पदान्तरे स्थित्वा । प्रकाशम्।) लदावलअ संदा वहारअ, आमन्तेमि तुमं भूओ वि परिमोअस्स । (इति दुःखेन निष्कान्ता शकुन्तला सहेतराभिः ।)

हृदय, प्रथममेव सुखोपनते मनोरथे कातरभावं न मुञसि । सानुशयविघटितस्य कथं ते सांप्रतं संतापः । लतावलय संतापहारक, आमन्त्रये त्वां भूयोऽपि परिभोगाय ।

Shakuntala *(to herself):* O my heart, even before, when the object of your desire came of itself so readily, you did not find courage (to accept it); why now this anguish when separated and (consequently) filled with repentance? *(Taking a step and standing still; aloud):* O bower of creepers who soothed my suffering, I bid you farewell, (hoping) to once more be happy (under your shade).

(Shakuntala departs in pain.)

—*Abhijnana Shakuntalam*, Kalidasa

For another Shakuntala,
as cussed and stubborn as this one,
and with grateful thanks to
Aman, Rashna and Ravi

0

Banaras; holy Kashi. The city of Shiva. The faithful arrive here in the hope of departure. To die in Shiva's city is to escape the remorseless cycle of reincarnation, to get away for eternity, be rid of it. Death lives here, forever mocking life and its passage.

I remember my first sight of Kashi: funeral fires blaze on the stepped ghats, inverting on the broken mirror of the waves. The low, sombre moon is tinted saffron with their heat. I do not see him, but Shiva walks among the dead, bending over to whisper the Taraka into the ears of corpses; his boat-mantra will liberate them, ferry them across the river of oblivion to the far shore of moksha.

Now, again, tongues of flame address the sky. The shadowed city clusters behind the glow and crackle of the pyres. Shakuntala died here, by the banks of this sacred river swollen by the rains. Yet I find no release.

The last of the depleted monsoon clouds stagger across the skyline. The wind drives the thin, tired rain, splattering damp ash on my face, lodging it in my hair. This fire-bed of scattered memory—how shall I deny it? She will not leave me, that Shakuntala. I carry her pain, and the burden of loves I still do not understand.

Always, the play of light from a wavering lamp upon a slate wall. Outside, water rushes over stones and rocks, past the sandy shore where a fisherman waits by a small fire. In the house, Shakuntala lies beside the man she loves. The rhythm of his breathing is enmeshed in hers. The smell of his skin is the fragrance of earth and sandalwood. She knows every hair on his chest, the way it curls, how it flattens before her approaching embrace. His face is in shadow, but his eyes, she knows, are quiet, watchful. She knows everything about him. There is love and understanding in this knowledge. There is sorrow.

What did he whisper in her ear when she clung to him? Now, I can only hear the peacock screeching, and the sound of the restless river echoing in the courtyard. A crow caws insistently, interrupting her thoughts, telling her something.

Light reflects on water, dazzling and blinding me, and I am transposed to another time, when the Ganga had shone just so. The river is cold under a late morning sun. Shakuntala can feel it lapping at her knees, tugging and pulling like an impatient child. There is a movement behind her, a soft splash and the sound of laughter. She turns and sees a horse at the water's edge, its forehead emblazoned with a patch of white. A man stands holding the reins, a stocky, muscular man, a traveller with irrepressible merriment in his eyes.

Later, a scarlet pennant fluttering and shivering on a spire of beaten gold, as the afternoon breeze follows the labyrinths and catacombs of the eternal city. Across the river, first sand, then forest. Temple bells howl and clang without reprieve. There is a wound in her womb, a stream of blood. She is dying. Convulsed by remembrance, by fear of recognition, she lies abandoned in Kashi, mocked by the indifferent glitter of the waves. A dog limps across the street and peers at her curiously. Sensing her pain, it settles beside her, like an ally. A procession of holy men in saffron robes marches by, a company of five. Is the sage Guresvara among them? Should his calm eyes meet hers, they would hold no horror, only denial. He has no pity, her brother.

In my dreams I see the jackal, his eyes searching the rushing waters, waiting to strike. Kali, her naked breasts covered only with a necklace of grinning skulls, keeps pace with him. Kali, fierce goddess, scavenger of desires, feasting on the refuse of dreams. Although she looks cruel, she is gentle; there is no pain in her realm, as there is no hope. But Shakuntala escapes her consolation and struggles upstream, to return to a life so thoughtlessly abandoned.

A lifetime hides in the space between these images.

What do we live for? Why do we die? To run away, always to run away from the self? Does the appetite for life become its own meal? Can the thirst of the river ever slake its waters?

I ask a priest on the ghats why these memories persist. He looks tired, perhaps bored. Notes and coins spill out from under the tattered rug on which he sits. His forefathers have perched by these weathered steps for thousands of years in this most ancient of living cities—older than history—recording the travels of pilgrims like myself. It is the first month of winter, but he wears only a limp cotton dhoti. The sacred thread is twined across his naked chest. He has flabby breasts and large, sightless eyes.

'You have been here before, sister,' he says, 'by this river, on these very ghats.' He scratches his underarms as his unseeing eyes contemplate the river. 'Our pasts live on. Each one of us carries the residue of unresolved karmas, the burden of debts we have to repay. Sister, you cannot run away. Confront this life. Only in acceptance will you find release.'

It is time for the evening aarti. The glow of prayer-flames reflects on the Ganga. Through the clamour of the gongs and conches I hear the howling bells. There is no silence between their ringing; even the echoes resound endlessly.

Shiva, it is said, is also Smarahara, the destroyer of memory. I died in his city, but I have not forgotten. How her body hungered and contorted, as she feasted on the flesh and threw the core away. Like a dhoomaketu, the tail of a comet, the debris of one life pursues me through birth and rebirth.

1

Meandering, the holy river winds through the month of Ashad. The hills gaze towards the distant plains. Trembling blue-green, the sky turns the colour of a lotus leaf. The still, late-summer haze holds the first premonitions of thunder.

I have run away to play in the forest, leaving my mother to her chores. Cushioned by the tall grass, I watch the hawks and eagles circle above and busy myself counting the clouds, assigning them shapes and names. I can see an elephant trumpeting in the sky, and a fluffed rabbit.

The clouds regroup, becoming a dark mass, ominous as fate. The world is closing in on me, shutting out the sky and all escape. I am paralysed with an unaccountable weight of despair, the kind that consumes one when everything seems about to end. I drown in cloud. A torrent of grief sweeps me in its flow. I flounder in a storm of deep-felt, incomprehensible rage. Streaked lightning mocks my fears. The rain, the thunder, the lightning, do they all know my sorrow, my despair?

Then the rain stops. From the wet and vanquished grass earth-smells rise in a steam. The cicadas begin their urgent, angry chant. The sharp showers have submerged an army of marching blue insects. Indragopa, they call them. Hoarse frog-gargles and harsh peacock laments assault my ears. Oppressed by the damp heaviness around me, the nagging memory of departed rain, I have ceased to cry. I am blank and stiff, weary from the constant plough of feeling. My flaxen skirt is soaked, streaked with mud, and when at last I make my way home, my mother strikes me thrice across the face.

'You wicked, heartless girl!' she shrieks. 'Were you born only to trouble and torment me?'

With wooden eyes I watch her as though from a great distance: her lined, sunken face, her trembling mouth, her chapped white lips edged with spit. I feel a pity for her that borders on disgust.

Again, the weight of my emotions breaks inside me. I shiver with more unshed tears. My mother tries awkwardly to embrace me, knowing that I will push her away. All night I sit on the worn oak threshold, confused by my anger and desolation. Between my keening and snivelling, the dawn lights up the eastern quarter with a sheet of gold, and I retreat to the narrow pallet in the back room to sleep.

I was named Shakuntala after the heroine of Kalidasa's classic drama. My namesake was not a mortal like me, she was a nymph, daughter of the celestial apsara Menaka who seduced the sage Vishwamitra and stole his seed. That Shakuntala had been deserted by her mother, and her birth-father Vishwamitra, and later by her husband Dushyanta—one could say that she carried within herself the samskaras of abandonment. Some even consider it an unlucky name.

It was my mother who named me Shakuntala. I never asked her why. She was no nymph or apsara, nor a learned rasika, but a rugged hill woman with a silent, dour passion for herbs and healing. My father had died when I was barely five years old, and his absence remained a stark presence in our unsheltered life. My first memories are of my mother diligently sorting herbs from among the weeds in our garden. My father had been a Vaidya, a doctor of medicinal plants, and she had learnt what little she knew about healing from him. The sharp whiff of amalaka, the sour reek of ashwagandha are irretrievably attached to these memories of childhood. My mother also tended our two cows, and the aroma of mountain herbs mingled in her clothes and her hands with the odours of milk and dung. I loved the cows, with their gentle eyes and grainy tongues, but while milking them I was always afraid that I would carry the same odour as my mother. The comfort of her bosom smelt rank, and I would recoil from her absent-minded embraces to run off and play in the garden outside our home.

We had few flowers in our modest garden, but there was a profusion of amalaka, tulsi, kantakari and other useful herbs. My mother would care for these in an order she had painstakingly learnt, intuited and improvised. The holy hemp, the pathya, was planted only at midnight on moonless amavasya nights, while the leaves of the black tulsi were never to be plucked on ravivara, the day of the sun-god. She tried to teach me something of this meagre knowledge but I resisted her attempts with an anger so violent that it sometimes surprised me. I hated everything about my mother, from her tangled hair to her shuffling gait and her cracked, dirty feet. I did not ever want to become like her.

I grew up in mountain country, like the Shakuntala of the epic. The hill people from our parts were called vanvasis, dwellers of the forests. It was a harsh life, of very few comforts, and our ways were far removed from those of the nagariks or cityfolk. We had little water to wash, for it was carried up from a great distance down the hill. Yet our house was always cold, or damp, or wet, as was the firewood, which burned badly and ruined our eyes. I often woke up with a hairy spider or an adventurous centipede sharing the pallet of lumpy straw on which I slept.

A fungal smell, compounded of stale gruel, smoke and disappointment, was settled like a pall about our house. Yet I stole my joys. All day I roamed the hills, where the forests abound with deer and stag, where tigers and panthers prowl. My mother had warned me to beware of the shalabhanjikas, forest spirits who enticed and enslaved young girls, but I loved the woods, and would return home reluctantly only when the shadows lengthened and the trees whispered like ghostly spirits. I was always cautious, though, and kept to the pathways and clearings. I thought I knew how to stay out of trouble, and was restless to see the world, to wander with the freedom of birds and clouds. I told my mother this and she sighed. 'Remember, Shakuntala,' she said, 'birds return to their nests at dusk, but clouds must weep their tears unseen in distant lands.'

Beyond the ridge, at the edge of the hill, was a narrow cliff. The young river hurtled below, a ribbon of rage, blue in summer, brown when the rains lashed the hills. I had improvised a rash game. I would run along the side of the cliff, contrary to the flow of the waters, until I was so giddy that I fell in a heap on the ground. I loved the edge of danger in this play; I knew well what could happen if I tumbled the other way. When the monsoons came, the earth was full of mud and slush. It was the blood-month of the river, when she was forbidden approach by mortals, and like the fishermen, I bided my time at home. I was also afraid of the leeches that appeared in this season; although my mother used them in her healing, the sight of blood sickened me. I waited impatiently for the monsoons to end. Then one year a goatherd fell off the cliff, where the earth had caved in. They retrieved his smashed body from a ledge far below only after the rains had subsided. After that I gave up the game, and began spending more time at home, to my mother's surprise and contentment.

I had a brother, only a year older than me. The astrologer who drew out his birth chart had foretold that he would someday be a great sage. My brother was called Govinda, meaning herder of the cows. He was a nervous child, afraid of the dark, waking me up at night with his silly fears. I would hold and comfort him against the demons of his imagining. 'I can hear death knocking,' he would whisper, while I knew it was only a woodpecker or a habitual night-beetle. Sleepily groping my way to the dark kitchen, I would find him a sweet modaka or ladduka, then murmur a comforting lullaby.

Later, after renouncing the world to become Guresvara, the man of dharma, did he ever remember those nights when he had lain tormented by anxieties and doubts? Perhaps he did, but he had fulfilled the astrologer's predictions by then.

I had another brother once. When my father died my mother had been left with his seed, and she carried him in her womb for close to a year. He was born different from us. He did not talk or laugh, and his wild eyes were focussed on things only he could see. His right leg was heavier than the left. When he first began to crawl he would drag the heavy foot after him. I worried about my brother; would he ever climb a tree, or walk up the hills? He had not crossed three summers when he was seized by the apasmara, the sickness inflicted by the dog-demons. His body arched and flailed, foam spilling from his mouth. Mother tried to heal him with herbs and prayers and invocations, but to no effect. He died before he learnt to walk.

We wrapped him in a shroud and went together to the river, where we bound his fate to a boulder and sank him into the water. My mother wept grudgingly, while Govinda I think was already so steeped in dispassion that he could only view death as deliverance. Sometimes, in my dreams, I saw my little brother, wrapped in a shroud, lying still below the unceasing motion of the river.

Govinda, whom I can now remember as anyone other than Guresvara only with an effort, was everything I was not. Even as a child, he knew, with the absolute conviction that characterized him, that he was a man of destiny, conceived only to restore order and true dharma to the world. My brother could be considered conceited. Born a Brahmin, descended from the Sapta-rishis, the seven sky-born sages, he was certain that the gods cherished him and acted and interceded on his advice. Constant as the North Star, the Dhruva-tara, his deeds and desires moved unerringly only in one direction, to save and preserve the ways of his forefathers.

These were troubled times for Brahmins everywhere. Govinda, parroting the gaunt temple priest who was his first guru, said that the deceitful faith of the Buddha had usurped the true path of the ancient religion. Disorder reigned, and kings, merchants, common folk all were overcome by the false piety of the new ways. Or so my brother claimed. I saw no error in disorder, it seemed to be the natural condition of life. Of course I kept my opinions to myself, for they were neither asked nor valued. My mother never fatigued of telling me not to fancy myself a scholar, as the scriptures were forbidden to women.

She worried incessantly only about her son, how she would oversee his education and ensure that he got the opportunities he deserved. Eventually, she managed to enlist him in a hermitage somewhere high in the mountains. The Rishi there was as renowned as he was learned. He had, however, only a handful of disciples, and it was a rare honour that my brother was included among them.

Every year, just before the monsoons, the traders and medicine men who wandered in search of herbs and healing plants held a great fair. The year that Govinda went to the hermitage, Mother, to my great delight, decided to take me to the fair with her. It was as if she had suddenly discovered me, now that the sun had departed and her eyes were not blinded by his dazzle. We trudged uphill for many hours through steep mountain trails, stopping overnight at a pilgrim shelter before we reached our destination.

The fair was held in the precincts of a Shiva temple. High deodar trees reached almost to the sky, banners and buntings strung across their sacred branches. An acrobat with blue scars on his face turned a series of giddying cartwheels to the applause of a cheering crowd. Pipes and bugles added to the merriment.

My mother bought me a doll. It was made of flax and wood, with seed-pod eyes and a sinister stitched-on smile. As she went off to examine the medicine stalls, I set about exploring the fairground, the doll cradled in my arm. Under an oak tree sat a man with a mess of matted hair and a snake, speckled, swollen with stillness, coiled around his ash-smeared neck. His wares were spread before him. I wandered around the stall in furtive circles, drawing patterns on the dust with my feet. The man was meditating, or perhaps alseep. But the snake followed my movements with inquisitive eyes. I edged

nearer. The oddest collection of objects was on display: birds'
eggs, owl feathers, crow beaks, raven claws, and a pile of
wriggling lizard tails laid out upon a black cloth, next to a
heap of monkey skulls.

A pretty yellow butterfly fluttered to rest upon the man's
serpentine locks. The snake coiled around his grey neck
swallowed the butterfly with a delicate hiss. The man's eyes
snapped open. 'Have you ever seen a snake charmer?' he
asked me in a deep voice, like a rumble, though I did not see
his lips move.

I shook my head in terror. 'Let me show you,' he said,
and led me to the far end of the temple grounds. My heart
was thudding with fear and anticipation. He took both my
hands and guided them to under his loincloth. I encountered
something wormy and wrinkled, and hit out at him with my
fists. His grip faltered and I fled. I turned once to see if he was
following me. He was sitting quietly under the tree again, the
snake circled round his neck, its hood erect.

Stumbling back in search of my mother, I sighted her
haggling animatedly with a trader in a wide, fur-rimmed Hun
hat. I broke into a panicked run. The acrobats had put up a
rope some distance away; I tripped over it and fell flat on my
face. I was bawling unashamedly, and the tears would not
stop. The doll's smile had come undone. A crowd gathered
around. 'She's lost!' someone exclaimed, 'the child is lost!' A
stall keeper distracted me with a ladduka, but I only wept and
choked the more while eating it.

Mother was utterly absorbed in her negotiations. The

acrobats beat on their Hurki drums, ceremoniously announcing that a child was lost and looking for her parents, but she did not register my absence. When at last she finished with her purchase and looked around for me, a perplexed frown knit her forehead into a tight jumble. I ran up to her, weeping. To my ultimate humiliation, she pinched my ear and marched me out.

I did not tell her about the man, or the snake, and what they had done to me. We began the long trudge back. When evening fell we were nowhere in the vicinity of the pilgrim-lodge where we had spent the previous night.

'Perhaps we are lost,' my mother said resignedly. They were the first words she had spoken since we left the fairground. We stopped to ask for directions. A group of villagers were gathered under a spreading bo tree. A woman draped in a flow of ochre robes sat cross-legged in the lotus asana, addressing them. Her shaven head looked strange, but not ugly, and the last rays of the setting sun cast a glow around her. We felt compelled to listen.

'I speak to you of Gautama, the one they call the Buddha,' she was saying. 'Gautama Buddha was the son of Suddhodana and Maya. Although he renounced the evils of the world, he did not renounce the world of women, for his mercy extends to all creation. The wife of Mahanaman was the first to receive the path of Dhamma.'

As the sun set, monks lit up lamps and incense around the bo tree.

'Good folks of the Sangha, do you desire to know more

of how the Buddha delivers his followers from the world of illusion?' the woman asked.

'Yes, we do!' the congregation answered in unison. My mother seemed interested in the sermon, though her brow was still gathered in a frown.

'Let me tell you of Princess Ratnavelli, then, who sent a letter to the Buddha through a group of merchants, asking him to teach her the path of Dhamma. The saviour responded to her call. He sent her a portrait, on which were inscribed the five prohibitions, the twelve nidanas, the three refuges. He listed out what was the truth, and the nature of untruth. The last sentence the Buddha wrote to her was: "Arise. Commence a new life."'

The audience was listening intently. 'What was it the Buddha said?' the Bhikkuni asked them.

'Arise! Commence a new life!' they replied together, as though in one voice.

We halted at the village that night, sleeping under a mulberry tree in company with other members of the Sangha. I awoke abruptly from my dreams before dawn, wondering where I was. The Sangha faithful were snoring like ogres. A lamp flickered under the bo tree. I pondered the preacher's words. 'Arise. Commence a new life.' What could it mean? How did one commence a new life unless one died and was reborn?

2

 We set off at dawn the next morning, returning home to find that my brother had come back as well. The great Rishi was too quick-tempered and demanding of his students. My brother had been found wanting. Shamed by his failure, he spent his time skulking in the fields around the village until mother found him a new teacher. A scholar who lived nearby was requested to teach him grammar, and coach him in the religious texts. All morning my brother would sit with this tutor, monotonously rehearsing the ritual pada-patha of the krama-patha, and the grammar of the jnana-patha, struggling with the perpetuation of learning which is the true task of the high-born mind.

Reluctantly coping with the drudgery of daily life, I would evade household work to eavesdrop on my brother's lessons. His tutor was an admirer of classical poetry. Between the declensions and conjugations of Sanskrit grammar and the stern abdications of the Brahma Sutras, we would get occasional snatches of verse and dramatic dialogue. It was through him that I first heard of Kalidasa, the great poet of Magadha.

While my brother was memorizing the mnemonic charts one morning, his tutor noticed me hovering by the door. 'What is your name, child?' he asked kindly. When I told him, his eyebrows shot up in pleasurable surprise. 'Shakuntala!' he exclaimed, 'the famed heroine of the greatest play ever written, *Abhijnana Shakuntalam*! Aah, the genius of her creator Kalidasa . . .' Closing his eyes, he rolled his head about as though spiralling into a trance. I stared at him in fascination. He had grey curly hair and an oily face. Emerging from his meditations, he found me peering at him, mouth agape. He winked reassuringly and did not seem upset by my scrutiny.

'Do you know the story of Kalidasa's play?' he enquired. I was silent, the desire to appear learned in conflict with my curiosity. He continued anyway, and told me of the virtuous Shakuntala, who succumbed to the love of King Dushyanta when he came to hunt in the forest. Dushyanta secretly married her, then returned to his palace, leaving her a ring as evidence of his love. But Kalidasa's Shakuntala carelessly lost the ring, and even though she was with child her royal husband disowned her and banished her from his court.

Just then, Mother called me in for some stupid chore. Govinda was back to the grammar lesson when I returned, and his tutor could only complete the story in broken fits and starts. The romance ended reassuringly, with Shakuntala's celestial parent Menaka interceding to put things right. I begged him to tell it to me again, but he never found the time.

Among her responsibilities, Mother carried the task of giving me away, but this was always secondary to her sacred duty to her firstborn son. I was eager to be married, for I saw it as an escape from the bondage of my situation. An unmarried girl did not merit a caste or a varna. Born to Brahmin parents, only upon marriage could I rise to the gotra of my husband's caste. Until then I was to help my mother with the housework, or tail Govinda as his tutor versed him in Sanskrit and philosophy and logic.

One summer's day, as I sat with Govinda and his tutor, a visitor peered in and amusedly observed us at our lessons. Later, my husband Srijan told me about how he had chanced upon a little girl struggling to make sense of her brother's tutor's instructions, and decided that, some day, when she came of age, he would marry her.

It was time for Govinda's upanayana, his 'second birth'. The man who would be my brother's new guru presided over the ritual with his acolytes. The monks fed the fire with logs doused in ghee and fragrant sandalwood. Govinda was dressed in his finest clothes, which my mother had kept ready in a frenzy of preparation. After the village barber shaved his skull smooth, leaving only the ritual topknot, his guru led him to a dark, smooth stone. Govinda stepped upon it, right foot forward, as the monks took up their chanting. 'Immutable and unmoving as the rock of dharma you stand upon, may you know and protect the true path,' they intoned.

Govinda was divested of his birth name, and all the

samskaras and memories that it carried. As he became the twice-born Guresvara, the sacred thread, the yagyapavita, was draped over his left shoulder and under his right arm. The priests began a sonorous recitation of the Gayatri mantra, after whispering it in my brother's ear. Mother plugged up my ears with her flaxen antariya. 'You can't listen to the mantra,' she told me, 'or else . . .'

'Or else what?' I challenged.

'Or else you'll grow a moustache and no one will marry you.'

My brother was a snataka now, a seeker of truth. The initiate changed out of his fine clothes into a renunciate's rough robes. The monks were presented with gifts, and a newborn calf. Guresvara accepted the blessings of his tutor and the village elders. A stern-faced priest arranged an antelope skin over his shoulders, and he was handed a staff of palash wood, which he held up level with his eyes. 'A life of penitence awaits you,' his guru declared, in an unnaturally loud voice. 'Pray, and proceed to beg for your living.'

This was the cue for Guresvara to bow before my mother and supplicate for food. As she filled his wooden begging bowl with uncooked rice, her sunken eyes brimmed over with tears. Then he came to me, his sister, for alms. Already instructed by my mother, I had a packet of fruits and jaggery ready. Guresvara looked so solemn, so absurd, with his shaven head and topknot, that I burst into a convulsion of nervous giggles. Mother leapt to inflict a cruel pinch upon my arm. The feasting began, with sweet and savoury dishes served to all in the village. As he prepared to leave, my brother's eyes met mine, and I was silenced by their contemptuous calm. And then we were alone, my mother and I.

It was a strange year. In the summer there were forest fires, flares of spiteful flame enveloping the green forests where I was accustomed to roam.

'The god Agni is showing his wrath,' Mother said fearfully. 'The villagers have forgotten to propitiate him, they have abandoned the fire-sacrifice, the old ways. The Buddha's Dhamma is good, but good alone is not enough to fight the ways of nature! We have to show gratitude to the gods.'

She passed her days silently staring at the harvest of fire, constantly examining the streamers she had strung around the house to read the direction of the wind. At night the skies were lit vermilion, and the tree trunks crackled and hissed until the dawn breeze fanned the force of Agni's angry breath towards the village. Snakes emerged from the fiery heart of the forest, crossing the intervening fields with anxious energy. A scorched rabbit ran into our house. I nursed it with devotion, but it died the same day. There was the smell of roasting flesh and indescribable menace around us. I had never known my mother to be afraid of anything, but now I read the fear in her face and in her muttered prayers, and this left me hollow with dread.

And then, one evening, Lord Indra's vajra, his bolts of lightning, his furious thunder, silenced the fire-god's wrath. It rained, and the flames were doused, while the scarred remains of the trees soaked in the downpour without gratitude. From the ashes, the leaves and blades of grass began to appear again.

Immediately afterwards, the locusts came, swarms of them, thick as the thunderclouds. As the day skies grew dark, we became accustomed to their constant buzzing, which was punctuated by a sullen, busy whir. The locust swarms seemed to move with some hidden internal purpose I could not decipher. I passed the daylight hours observing the patterns of their flight. It had been a wet and sticky monsoon, but the stagnant locust-air was even more stifling. They ate through the garden, destroying years of my mother's labour, they consumed the amalaka, the kantakari, the tulsi, even the pathya bushes—all of which she had tended and protected during the time of the summer forest fires. The woods, just recovering from the fires, were denuded of the hesitant new foliage, and stood as bare as when the first February winds had whipped and lashed them. The skeletons of trees mocked me in my dreams. Mother was resigned. It was difficult to be angry with the locusts, for they were only symptoms of our deeper, greater helplessness.

At last the gods grew gracious and the visitors began to die. They dropped ineffectually to the ground in heaps. The rain ponds were swamped with dead locusts, but at least the skies had cleared. There had been no birds after the fire, but now we saw a black mountain crow, and then another. The bears descended from the high forests to feed on the dead insects, and Mother forbade me to leave the house by night or day, for bears were known to carry away young girls and take them as their wives. At night we could hear them grunting and growling as they quarrelled over the locust morsels, while I lay rigid with fear on my lumpy pallet, wondering when the procession of horrors would end.

Guresvara's tutor appeared unexpectedly one morning, a rough bandage swathed over his arm. He had a wound that would not heal, and he had come to seek my mother's help. I was relieved to see him, his grizzly grey hair looked reassuring; he was a man, he would protect us from the terrible things around.

Mother opened his wound, which was congealed with blood and cloth and crawling maggots. She showed me how to soak the dried pathya leaves, then boil and strain them. Her broken teeth bit into her lips as she concentrated on cleaning the wound. First she seared it with an ember of wood coal, even as the tutor howled and groaned with pain. Then she left it for a day and a night, giving him a draught of herbs that glazed his eyes and dulled the pain. When he awoke we washed and dressed the wound. We tended to him eagerly, for it was good to have a man in the house again.

He stayed for several days, and spent his time teaching me, telling me stories. In the precious moments snatched from unending housework, I would listen to his talk. He recited poetry to me, from Kalidasa's *Ritusamhara*.

Clouds thicken the darkness of the night,
thunder peals loud and long.
Love-lorn women, their paths lit by lightning,
hide their faces as they rush to secret meeting-places.

I would follow the verse as he explained the matagayand chhanda, the poetic meter that mimics an elephant's majestic gait, swaying in time to its sonorous rhythm. The tedium of the everyday magically disappeared. When Mother, busy trying to bring her plants back to life, asked me to help her heap the garden with cow dung and dried grass, I did so. Humming verses from *Ritusamhara*, I had no fear that I would begin to smell like her.

One day I awoke to find that Guresvara's tutor had departed at dawn for his home in the neighbouring village. I was desolate. When in the evening I saw his lumbering form emerge from the evening gloom, I ran to greet him, and he held me in his arms. My mother appeared at the doorway, and he pushed me away, embarrassed.

He had brought us a book, the manuscript of Kalidasa's *Abhijnana Shakuntalam*. It was crafted of palm leaves, bound between two boards of engraved and painted wood. A design of water lilies had been worked into an elaborate border. I examined it with delight and a sense of trembling anticipation. 'We shall read it together, tomorrow,' he said. 'The poet Kalidasa was the brightest jewel in the court of King Vikramaditya of Ujjaini. Perhaps your mother would like to listen to the story of Shakuntala as well.'

It was a drizzly sort of day, the last of the monsoon rains subjecting us to their persistent misery. The thatch in the main room had developed a new leak, and my mother had placed a wide stone bowl under it to catch the water. The drip and plop of the leaking roof provided a sad backdrop for the moving tale that Guresvara's tutor recounted. 'A beautiful hermitage on the banks of the river Malini,' he began, and proceeded to narrate how the abandoned daughter of the immortal temptress Menaka and holy Vishwamitra was tended and cared for by the Shakunta birds. 'That's why she was named Shakuntala,' he explained. What would happen if I were to share her fate, I wondered. Would mother nature be as kind to me? He told us of how Dushyanta met Shakuntala and fell in love with her. 'The wild-wood bloom outglows the garden flowers . . .' King Dushyanta had exclaimed. The tutor looked into my eyes, repeating the verse, before he continued with the story of how the king married her in secret, by Gandharva rites. My stomach tumbled and turned in a flutter of unfamiliar sensations. He had barely reached the end of the first act, where a trumpeting elephant appears, fetters of trailing vines bound around its feet, frightening away the deer, when a man arrived from our storyteller's village with a message for him. 'I must leave,' said the tutor. 'I shall return soon and read out the rest of the play.'

That night, as I tried to sleep, I conjured the other Shakuntala, reclining on a bed of lotus leaves, by the vine-wreathed banks of the Malini River, writing a love letter to the king. I too was ready for love, eager for the exquisite sting of Kamadeva's arrows. King Dushyanta would surely arrive to claim me, his horses panting from the hunt. He would take me to distant lands beyond our unchanging hills.

The tutor didn't return for several days. I lay around in a simulated love-swoon, conscientiously avoiding the housework, and strangely, Mother was quiet. When at last he came again, he showed his arm to my mother. She pronounced that it had healed. 'You are well now,' she said. 'You should leave.'

3

 The seasons passed. Sometimes I would remember the Bhikkuni's sermon. 'Arise! Commence a new life!' she had said. My mind was filled with a vague disquiet when I remembered the words.

With Guresvara gone, my mother and I became companions, at least in the matter of running the house. I tended to the cows, mixing their feed, fresh grass, hay, sour milk and ginger, exactly as Mother instructed me to. While milking them I learnt to carefully direct the thin squirt of warm, white liquid towards the edges of the wooden pail. I scrubbed the cowshed to its cleanest, kneaded and patted the cow dung before plastering it in neat half-moon patterns on the floors and walls. In the afternoons, we sat together to sift the grain. Pausing at her work, her prematurely wrinkled eyes turning distant and soft with the pressure of memory, my mother would talk about her childhood in the high mountains. 'I was the most beautiful girl in our village,' she told me once. 'My long hair fell all the way to my knees.

When I braided it with forest flowers, everyone said that I looked like an apsara.' I did not believe her, but there was a wistful note in her voice which moved me, and I looked away to hide the mocking smile that had already spread from my eyes to my face.

I established an uneasy truce with my mother. She had grown fond of me, as though I were a pet parrot or a favourite calf. She indulged me in little ways, feeding me my favourite food, oiling and combing my hair. Sometimes, hesitantly, she would begin to talk to me, telling me about herself, but then something inside her would silence these confidences and she would frantically busy herself in some tedious, inconsequential household task.

'Tell me about my father,' I asked her. 'Who did he look like? Me or Guresvara?'

'Your father was only like himself,' she replied impassively. 'You look like me, while your brother's godly nature floods his face with such holiness that he appears the reflection of some divinity.'

It was a fond mother speaking, but I dissolved into jealous rage. Plucking all the marigolds in the garden, I stamped on them until they were interred in the damp earth. It was so like my brother, with his piety and noble ways, to intrude into my hard-earned happiness. Uncharacteristically, Mother didn't scold me for the ruination I had caused. Instead, she consoled me with a story her grandmother had told her in those long-ago times in the northern mountains. It was about a demon, a rakshasa named Uruvasura, who lived in a deep cave in the rock face. Every year, as the zephyrs of Vasant announced the spring, this monstrous creature would devour a virgin from the nearby village. Finally, when there were no more maidens left to sacrifice, a sorceress was deputed by the villagers to disguise herself as a young girl and keep his wrath at bay. Her magic, which, my mother said, was mostly flattery, so beguiled him that he married her and demanded no more ransom from the villagers.

'Did she enjoy being married to him?' I asked curiously, to which my mother replied that I had not understood the moral of the story at all. I told her I hated all stories with a moral, and prepared for another sulk. 'The lesson to be learnt is this,' she continued, holding my hand in hers and looking searchingly into my eyes, 'a woman must learn to read the hearts of men.' It was strange talk coming from my mother. I looked at her again. Perhaps she was beautiful once, and read the hearts of men. But I could not believe it, and I was not curious.

Guresvara was by this time attached to the guru Totakacharya, a favoured disciple of the most famous monk in India, the Shankaracharya. Their party was travelling through the hills near our village, on their way to the holy shrines near Badri–Kedar. The rules of his order discouraged novices from meeting their families, but his guru graciously allowed my brother to visit us.

I was playing in the clearing by the forest path that led to our village, skipping with the hemp rope which my mother had woven specially for me. I heard the sounds of loud chanting, as a group of wandering monks came into view. They were walking in step with each other, reciting a melodious prayer which matched the rhythm of their motion. The stately procession was headed by a tall man whose long strides and alert countenance gave an impression of strength and energy. Straggling at the end of the line of monks was a young boy who stopped to stare at me. A tuft of hair protruded from his shaven cranium and the ill-fitting ochre robe looked much too large for him.

I rushed to hug him, unaccountably happy to see him and eager to hear of the faraway places he had seen. But he withdrew awkwardly from my embrace. The others continued to march on, and had already progressed some way before they realized that one of their number was missing. They ceased their chanting as two of the monks retraced their steps to where my brother and I stood facing each other. The older of them turned unsmilingly to Guresvara and interrogated him harshly in chaste Sanskrit.

Guresvara explained that I was his blood-sister. The tall monk, who I later discovered was the guru Totakacharya, held up his hand in blessing. 'You can return home for a while,' he told my brother. 'Guru Sundaresvara will escort you. Remember, your mother is now your mother as all women are your mothers, your sister only as all women are your sisters. Be faithful to your vows and do not forget the discipline to which you are bound.' Guresvara smiled obediently, looking suddenly boyish, less like a shorn monk.

We returned home. My brother placed his begging bowl, his kamandalu, on the oak threshold and decorously took off his wooden sandals, placing them beside those of his preceptor, Sundaresvara. 'Hari Om,' he announced, his voice breaking as he spoke. 'We greet the lady of the household.' My mother hobbled to the doorway. The pestle with which she beat the rice had fallen on her toes two moons ago, and the wound was still congealed and infected. When she saw Guresvara, her mouth fell open and her bony hands fluttered to her face. He seemed taut and supple as a young bamboo plant as he bent forward to receive her blessings. She knew she should help her son observe his vows and merely blessed him, denying herself the comfort of holding him to her breast. But I remember that the effort brought tears to her eyes.

My brother's escort, the guru Sundaresvara, looked around disdainfully before settling himself upon the proffered asana, arranging his robes around him grandly as he held court. He had a habit of cracking his knuckles as he spoke which I found disconcerting in so holy a man. My mother did all she could by way of hospitality, offering him madhuparka, freshly prepared with curds, ghee, and honey, and the laddukas and jaggery sweets she had made for a recent festival day. He ate them indifferently, even ungraciously, and let out a loud burp.

With Guresvara back, my mother had no affection to spare for me. I found an abandoned childhood toy, my wood and flax doll with her battered seed-pod eyes, and wandered forlornly around the garden all morning, but nobody seemed to notice my absence. I would never treat my daughter so, I resolved.

That afternoon I was in the kitchen, searching for a sesame ladduka, when I felt the blood trickling down my legs. 'Something has bitten me, Mother!' I cried out fearfully. My stomach was racked by violent cramps, but I did not connect this with the blood; I had no sisters or aunts and I knew no young women who could have warned me. Mother came in from the front room. When she saw me, her face hardened. She twisted my ear sharply with her rough fingers and yanked me out of the kitchen. 'Have you no modesty, girl!' she hissed. 'Defiling the household fires when a holy man is visiting us! You are a woman now, you had better understand what that implies!' She dragged me to the low stoop beside the cowshed, her injured foot only adding menace to her angry march. Pushing me in, she secured the makeshift door with a narrow log. I lay on a pile of hay and grass, wondering what I had done wrong. The blood was flowing furiously, and I felt possessed by blind, flapping panic.

Even if I burst my lungs screaming, she would not hear me, my mother. An anger that had the feel and texture of helplessness rose within me, and I heard a scream emerge from some deep recess in my stomach. The sound fluttered like a torn pennant, defeated already in its purpose. I had been abandoned; I would bleed to death while my brother and his proud guru were plied with jaggery sweets.

I tried to reassure myself, but without conviction: Mother

would come, if only to check that the log bar in the cowshed was securely in place. Only last month, a goatherd had discovered the carcasses of two milch cows by the river. The villagers blamed the demoness who dwelt in the rock-caves near the cliff. The tigers did her bidding, as did owls and cats and other creatures of the night. This demoness hated the daily lives of ordinary people. Every year she took goats and cows and sometimes a child from the village to make her own. Then the menfolk decided to teach her a lesson. They pulled her by the hair and stoned her when she was passing by the fields one day. They tore up her clothes and spat on her face. She had not been seen around since, yet people were anxious about losing their animals.

But in her senseless joy over Guresvara's visit, Mother had forgotten our cows as well. I watched the daylight fade through the cracks in the door, and then, all of a sudden, I was on my feet, battering the door, throwing my body against it, till the plank that secured it splintered and gave way. I stumbled out, grazing my arm as I fell. Licking the wound, I tasted warm, salty blood. There was a sticky mess on my inner thighs. The thought and feel of the blood made me nauseous. But I would not go back to my mother. Driven by anger, by shame, by pride, I walked the reverse path, away from the home that had rejected me.

The moon had not yet risen; a glow hung over the forest announcing its arrival. I stood still awhile, straining to hear something, anything. Just as I became used to the unnerving silence, crickets and cicadas burst into shrill song. When I walked, the sound of my footsteps seemed to come from some other person following me. When I turned around to look, even my shadow escaped me.

The night was getting colder. The ground, the grass, the leaves that stroked my cheeks were all soaked with a pall of dew. When the moon rose, it cast unexpected, confusing shadows, but I trudged along, forcing one foot after the other, for it was now not my anger but fate that pushed me onwards. The hoarse croak of a raven, the frightened call of a sambal followed my path. I attempted to persuade myself out of my fears. Evil spirits lurked in the forest, I had heard—phantoms, spectres, disembodied souls—but so did good, kind spirits. What could the phantoms do to me, anyway? The earth-mother looked after all who were truly alone. And night was different from day only in the extent of what we could see or not see. When we were little, Guresvara had taught me how to whistle. I whistled to myself now, a happy, cheerful tune that gave me courage and indicated to anyone who might hear that I was not afraid.

Long into my trek, I saw a circlet of fire floating towards me. Slinking even further to the side of the path, I huddled against a damp rock. The vision descended to the level of my eyes, and I saw an unusually tall woman, naked but for a piece of coarse cloth around her waist, bend down and squat before me. She was slim and sinewy; her dark skin shone dully in the blue light of the moon. Removing the fire basket from her head, she placed it on the ground. The pungent scent of aromatic herbs hit my senses.

Her eyes, penetrating and rather amused, were illuminated by the glowing embers. Neither of us had spoken. She rose, picked up the basket of fire, and set off again, humming an obscure song. I fell into step with her quick, loping strides. Though I had never seen her before, I knew she was the rock-demoness, so hated and feared by the villagers; yet I followed her.

A clearing strewn with rocks and boulders led to an opening in the mouth of the hill. We crept through a constricted passage into a large, low cave where the air was thin and dry. The demoness brought out a bundle of firewood, from which she selected some twigs. Holding them against the sole of her foot, she broke them into smaller pieces. She placed these in the fire pot, blowing with deep careful breaths to build up a flame. As my eyes became accustomed to the dim light, I found her examining me from head to toe—my dishevelled hair, my bloodstained clothes, the ragged ankle-wrap already too short last summer. 'You have been blessed,' she said. Her voice had a slight metallic rasp. 'I see the blood-goddess has begun her sacred visitations on your body.' She took my hand.

A stream followed the winding curve of the rock wall towards some mysterious destination deep in the mountain. The rock-demoness led me towards it. Taking off my garments, I stepped in without shame. The warm, steamy water tasted of rust and blood. Suddenly, I was bathed in a pure, cool glow. I looked around in surprise and realized that I could sight the moon from a small aperture in the cave wall. The stream gurgled and lapped contentedly in the silver light. The moment passed, darkness returned. The demoness was standing by my side. 'Arise,' she whispered. 'May Raka, the goddess of the moon-night, transform you. Reap her knowledge!'

Obediently stepping out of the water, I draped my clothes around me. She combed and braided my hair, tied it up with a strip of old cloth, and offered me a stone bowl of roots and vegetables. I smiled at her in gratitude.

'Listen carefully, Shakuntala,' she said. 'I will instruct you in the ways of the goddess. Sometimes you will meet her as Kalika, or Raudri with the blue skin and eyes as yellow as a cat, who is the dark mistress of the illusory world. Do not be afraid when you sight her. And bow before her when you meet her as Jagat-Ambika, who is auspicious and beautiful and protects us all.'

'Are you really a demoness?' I asked apprehensively.

'Sometimes the goddess drips blood from her fangs,' she continued, as if I hadn't spoken, 'at other times she is a woman of beauty—her glances are her arrows, her eyebrows her bow; fragrant oils are her armour, her desire her chariot. Remember that in every one of her forms the goddess is always Swamini, mistress of herself.' Her words made little sense to me. I must have looked puzzled, for she put a hand on my shoulder, as an equal, and said, 'It is enough that you remember. Some day you will understand.' She wrapped me in a warm, soft rug and settled herself on a deer-skin mat. 'Let us sleep now, Shakuntala. In the morning I shall return you to your home.'

I did not wonder at her knowing my name. 'Do the tigers and panthers do your bidding?' I asked, emboldened by her kindness.

'I am a woman,' she said, 'though the villagers think me a sorceress.'

'And did you kill the cows in our village last month?'

'Everybody and everything dies,' she sneered. 'I take no credit for it. Each stone they throw at me multiplies into many more, and returns to hit and maim whoever has thrown it.' I frowned, trying to understand, and she smiled at me. 'You must be strong, Shakuntala. There is little place in your world for strong women, but none for the weak.'

Yawning with exhaustion, I was asleep in a trice. I suffered no dreams, no nightmares. 'It is time to return you to your home,' the demoness said when I awoke. We drank warm tea made from twigs and herbs brewed overnight in the fire pot, before she led me out of her cave. A weak half-light illuminated the landscape. In that liquid time of change the trees breathed like live things, and I was not afraid. By the time we reached the cowshed the sun had risen. 'Tell no one of our meeting, not even your mother,' she instructed, kissing me gravely upon my forehead with her cool lips, and in a flash she had disappeared into the woods. The animals rustled in the hay and mooed and grumbled as I settled myself on a pile of damp straw, waiting for my mother to appear, which she did, with a freshly washed pitcher and small lumps of jaggery for the cows. She seemed surprised to see me clean and groomed but did not say a word. Strangely, I felt no rancour. It was as if the previous evening had happened in a different life, and I helped her milk the cows in silence.

I spoke to no one of what had happened. In time I forgot the encounter in the cave; it blurred in my memory until I dismissed it as a delirious dream. Later, I wondered if running away was a talent I had been born with, or whether it was the rock-demoness who sowed the first seeds of self-destruction within me.

4

In the month of Magh the following year, I was at last wed to Srijan. It was a modest ceremony, for my mother was, after all, a poor widow, and my brother had renounced the world to become a Sanyasi. I wore silver toe rings and bangles, and a bead necklace of amber and lapis lazuli that had been in my mother's family for many years. Heavy gold hoops hung from my recently pierced earlobes, still raw with pain. My bridegroom brought me four ivory bangles and a double-stranded necklace of gold and black beads. The ivory bangles pleased me, I liked their cool touch, but I was not fond of jewellery. I found it cumbersome to wear and difficult to store safely.

In the month of Magh the skies are clear, although the days are still windy. The people in the hills fly parchment kites adorned with tails of straw and thin strips of cloth. The breeze holds them, lifts them up until they soar high with the hawks and kestrels. If I were a kite I could have fluttered in the wind and viewed all the lands below. I would have seen the sacred river that flows by our hills, until it meets the rocks, and the plains that stretch on and on until the end of the world. Now I was a bride, I had been instructed to look at the earth, to keep my gaze down and appear modest. Even as I garlanded my bridegroom, I looked down and saw only his feet. There was something in the way his toes gripped the ground which pleased me. I liked his feet, they bespoke strength and dignity.

I did not see his face until much later. The dusty palanquin, held by four sturdy villagers, was already carrying me to my new home when at last I ventured to look up. Our eyes met, and I was satisfied. His hand brushed my cheek, gently and a little inquisitively.

We did not lie together that night. On the first three evenings after we were wed, the women of the village staying in the house for the marriage rituals placed a rod in the middle of our marital couch. On those nights we were forbidden to cross the boundaries that this pole imposed. It was a tall piece of stripped wood, from the udumburu tree, anointed with sandalwood and robed with cloth. When I asked what it was, the womenfolk laughed knowingly. 'This is the rod of Visvavasu, the lusty Gandharva who claims the wives of well-born men,' they told me. We kept the tri-ratra vrata, and suffered Visvavasu in our lives. For three nights as the moon waxed we observed the vow of continence with which a true marriage must begin.

As we slept, the lamp by the door cast flickering patterns of light and shadow. It was an extravagance to keep an oil

lamp burning all night, but my husband seemed to think
nothing of it. He held my hand in his across the firm divide
of the udumburu rod. The steady rhythm of his breath lulled
me to sleep and I felt safe in the unfamiliar room with his
proximity and his touch.

When our time of waiting was over, Srijan mastered me
with courteous ease. In the years before my marriage, Mother
had stressed the demands of chastity. 'Never forget, the vessel
of your virtue is like the urn of water you balance on your
head,' she would say. 'You must not spill even a drop as you
carry it home!' Her talk had only confused me. When I lay
in my nuptial bed, I understood at last what she had meant;
I understood what was possible. Our bodies knew each other,
and his touch brought me alive. After the rod of Visvavasu,
which had divided us, was removed, his hands travelled to
every crevice of my body, warming me, flushing me, filling
me with joy. It is all so long ago now, I am no longer the
same person as that young girl who yearned to soar like a
Sankranti kite in the windy mornings of the month of Magh.
Yet I carry in my bones the feel of Srijan's hands, the heat of
his breath on my body that first night.

Srijan had known me since I was a child. He had noticed me
during the grammar lessons with my brother, when he came
to our village to settle a dispute, and marked me out as his
bride. I was his third wife, but everyone said that I was the
most beloved. In any case, his other wives were dead and had
not given him any children. I had no mother-in-law to

torment me and no father-in-law to serve. I enjoyed a rare degree of freedom for our times. I could swim in the river when I pleased, climb the trees in the forest in search of bird nests, rest in the grassy meadows to stare at the sky and dream. When evening fell I lay in Srijan's arms, in the warm room where oil lamps flickered. The sound of the river, sobbing or sighing or singing a tuneful melody as the seasons dictated, could be heard through the long nights we dedicated to love-making.

There were no barriers between us, no boundaries to our joy. We would sport and rest and sleep, awakening to return once more to our love-games. Playing hide-and-seek with our kisses, we would find ourselves lost in our reflections, each in the other, and then in the reflections of the reflections. This category of kiss, Srijan told me, was known as the pratibimb, or the mirror, and it reflected the true philosophy of love. I told him that true love had no philosophy but the joy that gave it sustenance. 'You surprise me, Shakuntala,' he laughed and asked me where I had learnt such a thing, but I did not know that myself.

Every morning when dawn broke, a kokila warbled outside our room. 'Kuoo,' it would say, 'kuoo, kuoo!' As its call rose to fever pitch, Srijan would awake and sleepily kiss me to mark the new day. My husband was a mahasamant, a rich man, the chief of fourteen villages. He had herds of bullocks and cows, buffaloes and she-buffaloes, rams and ewes. He was a serious man in his everyday affairs, a person of learning and discrimination, but when we were alone he would bite and tickle like a truant youth. We feasted on all our senses, and yes, certainly, we were happy.

On our wedding night my husband had led me to the courtyard behind the house. The moon shone bright and clear in the sky, and there were few stars visible. 'Look beyond that tree, Shakuntala,' Srijan had said, holding me by the shoulder, guiding my line of sight to the leafless branches of neem, just about to break into new flower. 'Beyond that tree, above the mountain, you can see the star of Arundhati. She is the purest of wives, the emblem of fidelity. As you see that star by my guidance, so I shall guide you in our life together towards the vision of right and wrong.'

It was merely a ritual, and my husband never believed overmuch in ceremony. Yet the sight of the Arundhati star made me thoughtful, even apprehensive. 'I cannot see the star,' I lied, 'and besides, my head is hurting.'

I could never understand rituals, why some things had to be one way rather than another, why a twig on the sacrificial fire must point to the right rather than the left, why a woman who was menstruating was unclean, why games had to have rules. Who made these rules? Things were as they were, and would remain so however strange or absurd they seemed. I resisted these certainties, just as I pretended not to see the star of duty towards which my husband pointed me.

Although the ancient gods still ruled our hearth, Srijan did not believe excessively in anything. He told me once that he had seen too much of the world to burden himself with convictions. My husband had travelled far into the north where the Huns lived, to the distant south, and even to the lands of cannibals and barbarians in the east. He was by nature trusting, never tormented by doubt or suspicion. Srijan's mother had taken the path of the Buddha. She had become a nun and shaved her hair before she died, but her son had reverted to the ways of his forefathers. The battle of the religions seemed not to affect him.

I never met Srijan's mother. The kitchen maids Dhania and Kudari murmured and whispered about the story of her life. Long ago, a party of travelling monks of the Buddha's faith had come to the village. There were nuns and women initiates among them. I had heard it said that the head lama cast a spell on my mother-in-law. She had been pounding grain in the backyard when the call came. She left the task half-done, the unhusked akshata on the floor, the half-pounded saktu still in the mortar, the pestle abandoned in the garden. The Sakyamuni had summoned her with his teachings and she left her world to follow him. She had a husband and a young son, a home and a kitchen. What was she searching for, why did she go away? She spent the rest of her years with the faithful of the Sangha in a monastery. Srijan never talked about his mother, yet her departure must surely have caused him pain.

Gautama Buddha was a prince of the Sakya tribe. Perturbed by the problems of life and death, the sorrows of the human state, he decided to set forth as a homeless wanderer in search of the truth. The Buddha escaped his palace walls to see and taste and feel the curious wonder that the world is. Perhaps

Srijan's mother, too, had renounced the world to do just that—to find it. 'Arise. Commence a new life,' the Bhikkuni had said. I think I was, even then, envious of my mother-in-law and her hard-won freedom.

My own mother had died soon after my marriage—quietly, I was told, in her sleep. I thought of her as enjoying whichever of the heavens she was traversing or, already reborn, suckling at some new mother's breast. I had long forgiven her nagging, her unspeakable partiality to my brother, swallowed those hurts and jealousies like a bitter potion, a medicine which strengthens. I still remembered how she pounded the herbs until a line of sweat formed upon her crumpled upper lip, how she scoured the forest undergrowth for plants and leaves and bark. A pilgrim had once told her of silajita, a medicinal extract obtained from a particular type of mountain rock. Some months before she gave Srijan permission to claim me, we had set off together up the cliff face in search of it. I recalled her anxious frown as I clambered up in the futile quest. It was a steep incline. I felt the loose soil crumbling as a rain of small rocks fell hurtling below my feet. Frightened, I hung on to a rooted bush and continued to climb. Something in her spirit, her mute courage, had challenged me to carry on. I had loved my mother, in my own stubborn manner, and now that she was gone, perhaps I understood her.

5

If you were to climb to the top of the hill behind the house of which no trace remains (but I remember), if you were to walk straight along the path that follows the spine of the mountains and then climb down again for a while, you would reach the ruins of a circular temple. It was once dedicated to the mothers of creation, the Matrikas, the unfettered ones. They were restless goddesses. Tired of living within the confines of the temple, they had left it behind and moved on, no one knew where. So it was, even then, already a place that the priests and the gods had forgotten. No bells rang there, no incense was lit, no prayers chanted.

I went often to this abandoned temple, and sat in the shadow of the wooden pillars where the swallows sheltered, listening to the lazy rustle of the afternoon breeze. I would look at the sky and think of nothing, sensing in my heart that there were thoughts and events and people that beckoned. What had sparked such wild, dangerous dreams I could not say. Perhaps it was my husband Srijan and his tales of travel, or simply the consequence of a foolish, imaginative and reckless nature. I was hungry for experience. There were things I wanted to see, to know, to do. My ignorance irked me; I had, for example, never actually viewed an elephant. I had heard that the mrighastin, described as the beast with a hand, was the noblest and wisest of animals. I recognized it from representations—on a carved urn, in the frame of a polished brass mirror. Sometimes I even dreamt of these mrighastins, as the Buddha's mother had done. 'How many tusks does an elephant have?' I would ask Srijan, although I already knew the answer, or 'Is an elephant's tail more like a cow's or a monkey's?'

Soon after I was married, an elephant had ventured up the steep mountain paths that led to our village, dislodging stones and boulders in the course of its ascent. Incoherent with excitement, I babbled on about how I would feed it jaggery, and persuade the mahout to let me ride through the forest, eye level with the trees. But that very night I was visited by the ritu, the monthly curse of women, and for the next four days I was relegated to the inner room, so as not to defile the household. The hated confinement threw me into deeper depression than ever before. All the women of the village went to observe the spectacle. The maid Dhania reported that she had fed the visitor with sesame sweets and it had blessed her with its trunk.

However, the precipitous mountain paths around our village were too narrow to allow it passage, and the mrighastin continued to cause landslides wherever it went. A pregnant woman died in such an accident, and her enraged relatives beat up the mahout. He and his elephant in turn beat a hasty retreat to the dusty plains from where they had arrived.

By the time I had washed my hair and purified myself, the great beast was already gone, returned to the distant lands I glimpsed from the hilltop on my way to the temple. No other ever ventured our way. I wept that night, and not even Srijan's passion could release me from the prison of my rage and regret. I made him promise to take me with him on one of his long journeys. To humour me, he said that he would some day. I did not believe him.

Although many men and horses and palanquins passed by the mountain paths that led to the high passes, there were few visitors to our home. This was the pilgrimage route to the sacred shrines of Panch-Badri and the peaks of the Gandhamadana Mountains. The herdsmen who took their cattle for summer pasture knew these paths well, as did the itinerant medicine men and traders in rare mountain herbs who jealously guarded the secrets of their routes. The people of the Hun lands used the paths to trade for sugar and borax. Gold was bought and sold at the passes, and much else— silver, jewellery, wool, musk, elephant tusks, rhinoceros horn, strong medicines, even secret poisons from the land of the Bonpas. But the mingling of men and exchange of riches happened far from our quiet hamlet. We had no need for trade. The villages around us cultivated corn and millet, and sometimes rice. It was a self-contained world, into which only the pilgrims and traders occasionally brought news of the larger world.

I knew there was more inside me than the limits of my experience dictated. I thirsted for glimpses of new lands, people, ideas. It was as if the move from my mother's home to my husband's—the half-a-day journey from one village to another—had suddenly made the impossible possible. A man's equal in bed, why could I not desire what men enjoyed: the freedom to wander, to be elsewhere, to seek, and perhaps find . . . *something*?

I found that I could argue with the scriptures, if only in my mind. The first verse of the Brahma Sutra begins, 'Atha ato Brahma jignasa . . .': 'Now there is sincere desire for knowledge of the ultimate.' But knowledge of the ultimate cannot be gained without knowledge of the intermediate. My brother Guresvara had studied philosophy under an Advaita guru, a follower of the Shankaracharya. He had interminable debates at the monasteries with learned Buddhists and other disbelievers about the true nature of the self. 'What is the self?' they would query self-importantly. 'Is it the body? Is it the mind? Is it the ego?' I, Shakuntala, would have told them that it is none of these: the self is a seedling, a core, which observes, experiences, and persists even when everything else changes and passes.

'The instinctive belief in the selfhood of the body is a primal error,' my brother Guresvara had told me primly. If he had listened to me I could have explained that just as I knew he was my brother and Srijan my husband, I knew that

I was I. The self that perceives the similarities between the past and the present, the self that does not forget, the self that is present in time, is me.

As always, thinking about my brother Guresvara, who was once Govinda, left me dissatisfied.

During his travels to the east, Srijan had met a soothsayer who urged him to perform the Agnicayana ritual so that the new woman of his house might bear sons. Anxious for an heir to light his funeral pyre, my husband decided to initiate the prayers. Despite his professed disbelief in ritual and ceremony, he sent for priests from distant Kashi, inviting them to our mountain home to conduct the Agnicayana. I was painfully aware that I had been lagging in my duties as a wife. Every month my ritu would arrive and prove me barren; Srijan's seed would not prosper within me. I was at fault, yet I resented the knowing looks and arch insinuations of the women of the household. Although Srijan was too kind to show his disappointment at my infertility, the Agnicayana ritual was another bitter reminder of my inadequacies.

I consoled myself that the prayers might provide a change from the dull routine of everyday life. 'Will they bring an elephant for the ritual?' I asked. Srijan laughed indulgently. 'You shall receive new garments and gold and silver ornaments and the blessings of the great gods,' he told me. 'Is that not enough to please you?'

'No, I want to see an elephant!' I persisted.

Srijan looked at me with laughter in his eyes. 'You are an

odd woman,' he said. 'You do not care for ornaments or rich garments or a man's flattering words.' He said this gently and without anger. Looking back, I think perhaps he liked this about me. And still I could not be consoled about missing out on the elephant, not for all the gold and gems and garments in the world.

The priests who were to conduct the Agnicayana ritual arrived from faraway Kashi, the golden city by the banks of the Ganga. The Adhvaryu, a pompous man responsible for performing a majority of the rites, managed to unnerve me the most. The Hota, who was to recite from the Rig Veda, and the Udgata, who chanted from the Sama Veda, were also from the holy city. Dressed in soft silk robes more suitable for courtiers than priests, they spoke Sanskrit in an affected style, and constantly flapped their dhotries this way and that. Their pretentious, hypocritical talk infuriated me. Hoping to amuse Srijan, I imitated their mincing ways. He reproved me for this irreverence. 'The life of a householder is different from that of a holy man,' he said gravely. 'A lady of the household is bound by duties quite distinct from those of a priest or monk! Perhaps you are forgetting who you are.'

What was it about the learned priests from Kashi that angered me so? I was no uneducated hill woman who knew only how to clamber on to rocks or climb trees! My brother Guresvara was a revered monk. Although we did not use the high language of prayer and ritual in our daily speech, I too had learnt how to construct declensions and conjugations in Sanskrit, been taught the proper mode of address for men, beasts and objects. I told Srijan this, but he only laughed and said he knew he had a scholar for a wife.

A terraced field just above the river, which had lain fallow for some years, was selected by the priests as the site for their recitations. I observed them establish the four directions: north for the god of wealth, south for the god of death, east and west for prosperity and plenty. As they set about calculating the four quarter-directions, and confabulating on all sorts of details of the rituals, the village priest listened awestruck, his mouth hanging open in admiration. He had evidently not encountered such wisdom before.

The chief priest, the Adhvaryu, called me aside. 'When did you last have your monthly blood-visitation?' he asked, in a tone both contemptuous and accusing. 'Your impurity would defile the ritual, take away its merit.' I was tempted to lie and disrupt his prayers, but I was a well-born Brahmin woman. There were some things I could not do, try as I might. So I told him the truth, that it was now six days since the ritu had departed. I had washed my hair and bathed myself with the appropriate invocations; I was pure and could offer my body, mind and soul to the great forces beyond. The Adhvaryu was not convinced, and stared at me with suspicion. The cast of his lips set his face into a perpetual sneer. 'The field of your body resists your master's plough,' he said. 'Be sure that you will be pure during the prayers.'

That night, as we made love to each other, I clung to my husband as though I might lose him. His chest was matted with soft hair, like a lion's mane. I lay with my head against his heart, and listened intently to its rhythm. In the distance, the sacred river roared as it fell from the moon on Shiva's brow. I heard an owl hoot, and in the distance a pack of jackals, howling. According to the words of the wise these were not propitious sounds, but I knew and loved the owl that sheltered in the mulberry tree behind our house, and as for the jackals, did they not share the great universal soul, partake of its consciousness?

The day of the Agnicayana, I rose early and chose my clothes with care. Wrapping the scarlet silk uttariya neatly around my waist, I draped it over one shoulder and under the other until it artfully followed the curve of my breasts. My ankle-length antariya was of fine Cheena silk dyed a flattering shade of indigo. My bracelets and anklets had been freshly polished. Painstakingly positioning the snake-shaped kamardhani around my waist, I suspended my antipathy to the learned priests from Kashi, and proceeded to the altar with the confidence of a well-loved woman secure in her beauty.

Srijan entered the ritual enclosure, holding the ukha pot containing the household fire aloft in his arms. His eyes did not meet mine. He walked carefully, and his brow was balanced in intense concentration. The Adhvaryu took two pieces of flint and struck them together with an inaudible incantation until a spark of fire flew from his hands to the altar. This was followed by a second incantation and another faint spark, but it was still necessary to extract an ember from the ukha pot before the fire sprang to life. I smiled and twirled my uttariya and tried to catch Srijan's eye, but he did not seem to notice.

The long recitations and invocations left me yawning. I awaited the concluding verse from the Rig Veda, 'May Agni, the divine fire, lead the offering to the gods.' This was my cue and I was ready for it. I took the cakes of rice and barley that the priests had prepared on the household fire and handed them to my husband. Srijan placed them on the altar. 'For Agni, the divine fire, not for me! All action, all joy, all pain, is for Agni, the divine fire, not for me!' he declared. The fire crackled and hissed, and cast an ochre glow on my husband's calm face, which looked suddenly like that of a stranger.

The monotony of the prayers did not let up. I tried to hear the river, but it was drowned by the loud, ceaseless drone of the priests. Twelve sacrificial goats were tethered to the trees outside the enclosure. Eleven of them pattered in with tenuous dignity to the sounds of timid bleating. The village priest, the lowest in the hierarchy, was assigned the task of slaughtering the goats. He did this swiftly, without remorse. The sandy soil was stained with blood. The smell and sight of it sickened me. I was overcome with nausea. Srijan noticed my plight, and reached out to hold my hand. The Adhvaryu restrained him. 'Confine your thoughts to the ritual, sir,' he said harshly.

The chanting continued. The sponsor of the ritual, the Yajamana, had to be consecrated. Srijan was instructed to bend down on his haunches and crawl into the skin of a black antelope, which had been set up in a sort of tripod for this purpose. He emerged wearing the dark hide upon his broad shoulders. A silk turban was tied around his head by the

Adhvaryu. He was given a staff, a rough stick of stripped wood, and instructed to close his fists. I found it all comical and yet somehow frightening. Everything that was dear and familiar had been rendered suddenly strange and alien. Srijan arose, holding the pot filled with fire. Sloughing off the black antelope skin, he donned a glittering gold breastplate, which quite covered up the greying hair on his chest. I rose with him, and together we circled all the fires, the household altar, the sacrificial altar, the southern fire, swearing our faith and constancy to them and to each other.

The black, acrid smoke billowing from the sacrificial fire, my husband's face shimmering in the haze, the priests croaking on and on like monsoon frogs, the smell of milk and blood on the damp soil: I was tired of it all. I longed for the consoling rituals of my own daily life.

All night I lay hungry for my husband's rightful love. Stirred in my dreams by visitations from the Ashvins, the lustful youths of the morning wind, I reached out for Srijan. He restrained me. 'No, Shakuntala,' he said, 'it is forbidden. We must do as the priests instruct.' The cruel rod of Visvavasu had once again reasserted itself in our marital bed.

The pot containing the sacrificial fire was buried underground, and barley seeds sown on the soil above. The long delicate stalks of Soma were then soaked and left to ferment. On the tenth morning the pressing of the Soma wine began. The first oblations were offered to all the different gods. The newly pressed wine smelt of earth and honey. Sipping it, I felt an exaltation I had never before experienced, a limitless freedom. Like the bird in the sacrificial altar, I too could soar across the sky.

The priests were gifted with gold and cows and clothes before they disbanded. I too was given presents—silks and ornaments, a peacock-feather fan with a jewelled handle. The twelfth goat, the one not offered for sacrifice, was let free. It looked confused, bleating piteously as it scrambled off towards the fields.

'I would like to drink Soma wine every day of my life,' I whispered to Srijan, as we lay together. I had not been with him for ten nights, and yet he did not respond to my seductions.

He sat up, perturbed by my talk. 'Please understand this, my beloved Shakuntala,' he said. 'The real Soma, the nectar of the immortals, is already lost to humans. We drink the substitute elixir of our times. Soma wine, like knowledge, or love, is only appropriate when offered to the gods. It is a libation, a part of the order of the universe. By itself, it turns to bitter poison.'

We did not resume our love-making. The next morning, Srijan left again for the lands of the east. After his return, it was never the same again. When I try to recall the texture of that life now, I forget his face; I can see his night-eyes, but the exact cast of his features eludes me. I remember only the antelope skin, and the gold breastplate covering the grey hair on his chest, as we invoked the gods to drink the Soma wine.

6

The time that my husband was away passed slowly. Restless, I consoled myself by applying collyrium in my eyes and alta on my feet. I rehearsed the fourteen kinds of seduction I had surreptitiously studied from the forbidden palm-leaf texts in Srijan's collection. I chatted with the hunchbacked fisherman who sat all day by the river and watched him reel in his catch. I observed the river crabs scuttling in the sand and wondered what they thought of our world, of my alta-coloured feet and silver anklets set with parrot-green stones. I climbed a tree just to stay in practice, and in a fork in the branches I discovered a cuckoo's nest with eggs in it.

I went to the field where the Agnicayana ritual had been conducted, and saw that it had finally been ploughed. No blood or bricks or Soma remained. Thinking of my husband, in his antelope cloak and glistening gold breastplate, I was lonely without him. 'I am Shakuntala, the wife of mahasamant Srijan,' I told myself, 'and I am happy to be her.'

'I will conduct myself befittingly,' I resolved, and returned to the house to check the stocks of rice and barley and sorghum. They were all in order, for the household ran smoothly with or without me. So after supervising the cleaning of the cowsheds I made my way to the abandoned temple beyond the ridge of the mountains and lulled myself by thinking of nothing.

It was the afternoon before Srijan returned from his travels. As I sat on the stone steps leading to the temple, my mind was easy and my body glad. The shrine was surrounded by a grove of oak trees, which are sacred, oracular beings. They attract lightning, and villagers have always both venerated and feared them. A woodpecker was perched on a gnarled branch, knocking at the trunk in search of water. A crane flew by, its moon-white wings gleaming against the deepening shadows of the sky. A snake glistened and slithered around me before disappearing down the steps. These were good omens. Srijan would return safely from his interminable journeying. This evening would be different from all those that I had whiled away in his absence.

When I reached home my husband had indeed returned from his travels. He had brought back a woman with him. She was standing by the doorway as I entered. Something about her, her clothes perhaps, reminded me of the peacock-feather fan I had received as a gift. With her elongated neck and tall, arching figure she looked like a crane in flight. Her eyes, when they met mine, were like a serpent's.

Srijan did not have much to say about the woman. 'Do

not ask any questions, Shakuntala,' he entreated. 'She has been brought here as your handmaiden, and that is all. See that you treat her well.'

'I shall be glad to be of service to you,' the woman said politely, though her voice had no trace of surrender. But it was melodious; the twanging of a tautly drawn veena string. I felt clumsy and awkward. And, yes, inescapably jealous.

Covering up my confusion with a bright false smile, I avoided Srijan's eyes. He avoided mine. Quietly, I left the house and retraced my steps up the long, steep path to the Matrika temple. It was the only place where I could hide, cower in shame and examine the new reality that confronted me. I was not angry with Srijan—he was a man, men were allowed many women, it was the way of the world as I knew it. But the hurt and betrayal, the prickling of thorns under the sheath of my skin—I had never known or anticipated these feelings, just as I had never expected my husband to return from his journey to the east with an exotically beautiful woman with cold and mocking eyes.

I had known rage before, and anger, when, as a child, my mother had favoured my brother over me. But this was worse, a collapse of all that had been good and true in my life. I screamed and sobbed aloud, beating my head against the stone walls of the temple like the kind of woman I had not imagined I would ever become. The sun had set over the deodar trees, and the sounds of the forest mingled with the silence of night. I was not afraid. I felt safe, even secure, in my fierce despair and loneliness. That is the thing about tears:

if you cry loud and deep enough they become a form of comfort.

I wondered if Srijan was worried, if he was searching for me. I could picture him, brows folded in perplexity, lips clenched tight and eyes stern to conceal his fears. Srijan was a soft man, a kind man. I knew how to handle him. He would send her away, this temptress, usurper of my joys, and when I returned I would kiss and fondle him and we would make love to each other all night. My husband had done nothing wrong, he had not hurt or scorned me. He had brought a woman home from his travels to work as my maid and do my command, but she had looked down at me from a great height and viewed me with contempt. It was not his fault.

The shadows crept in. It was time to return home. I thought of Srijan and how anxious he must be. The thought made me glad, eager to see him again. But I was suddenly afraid of the dark night, and the wild animals that might attack me on the lonely walk back. I did not have the courage of my childhood. It was a cold, clear night. The north wind was like a knife. The circular temple was roofless and open to the heavens, where the constellations glittered and shone, each in its place. It was too dark to distinguish the pillars and colonnades around the central platform. They must once have framed images of the Varahis, Mahavidyas and Dakinis. Learned Yoginis must have worshipped here. Why had the goddess abandoned her temple? Where had she gone?

Huddled by the wooden pillars, I could dimly distinguish a low opening, lit by an oil lamp. A shaft of light fanned out from behind a crevice in the worn stone. Groping around in the dark until I reached the edge of the platform, I found a break in the wall on the other side, through which I managed somehow to slip in. It was a narrow, circular passage that led to an enclosed chamber. This was surely the garbhagriha, the womb of the temple. The lamplight cast shadows, moving like ghostly women in a slow dance. The floor was not of our local slate but a darker, smoother stone. The yoni, symbol of the goddess, was engraved upon it. Concentric lotus petals were carved around the yoni, overlaid by offerings of old flowers, leaves and petals. Could Dakinis and Yoginis still be worshipping here? Did spirits of the netherworld pay tribute to the goddess in this secret space?

I felt protected in the garbhagriha. As I reclined on the stone floor, the terrible events of the day began to recede from my memory. A sense of ease invaded my body, and I felt drowsy, languid. It was as though I was back in the cave with the rock-demoness, the time when I had first run away. In my sleep I was talking to someone. As I awoke I heard my own voice, not heavy after a night's dreams but loud and clear, caught in mid-sentence: '. . . and her glances are her arrows,' I heard myself say, 'her eyebrows her bow; fragrant oils are her armour, her desire her chariot.'

The lamp was not yet extinguished. An infinitesimal point of light balanced steadfastly on the edge of the wick. A blanket of freshly plucked flowers lay on the yoni, young blossoms of bakul and harsringar, madhumalti and honeysuckle. Where had they come from, who might have brought them?

Peering back behind me one last time before departing, I saw that the lamp had at last been snuffed out.

It was still the time of the half-dawn, when the Ushas, the daughters of heaven, first light the sky. I waited until the Ashvins and the Maruts and the seven horses of the sun-god began the march of day. Only when I could feel the golden rays of the sun on my skin did I venture back home.

I found Srijan pacing outside. He was stroking his beard, as though to calm himself. When he looked up at me and was silent, my heart sank, and tears welled up in my eyes, provoked by relief as well as fear. 'I got lost in the forest,' I said in a rush. 'It was an amavasya night. No moon shone in the sky to guide me home. It was too dark to return and I was afraid of the bears.'

'Where did you spend the night, Shakuntala?' he finally asked.

'Sheltering in the branch of a walnut tree,' I lied. 'I was awake all night, I couldn't sleep a wink!' I am not a good liar, so to cover up I started weeping once again, as much at having to lie as at everything else.

The woman was not to be seen. I retreated to our chamber and lay down, suddenly tired. Outside, the river beat and crashed relentlessly against the boulders and rocks by the shore. She was angry today. A crow with beady, inquisitive eyes cawed by my window. I stared back, blank, silent. The strength that had swelled up inside me in the temple had quite disappeared. I felt silly and inconsequential after the meaningless rebellion of the night. I knew my behaviour was sulky and childish, but I could not control it. I hated her.

The tinkle of silver anklets alerted me. I turned around to see her framed in the doorway. She was wearing an immaculately pleated antariya. She was slim but large-boned, with long feet that looked elegant despite their size. There was a balance and symmetry to her build that was very seductive. I could not imagine her milking cows, or washing clothes, or doing any of the things that must be done in a rural household like ours.

'I have a soothing balm for your forehead, and unguents for your body,' she said, in a low voice that seemed designed for whispered confabulation and the sharing of secrets.

'No,' I said rudely, 'there's nothing that I want. Leave me alone!' She slithered out of the room. I didn't even know her name. I wanted to know nothing about her.

That night I lay in our bedchamber awaiting Srijan's arrival. When at last he came in, he seemed troubled and preoccupied. We lay together awkwardly, the silence of strangers settling over us. I was stiff with tension, and the muscles of my back were aching. I wanted to touch him, but I could not. My questions lay between us, just as the rod of Visvavasu had in the first days of our marriage. Srijan slept, but I was awake, although I lay motionless so as not to disturb him.

I spent the following day by the river, feeling the wind in my hair. I conferred with the fisherman, Kundan, whose eyes were less shadowed than on other days, perhaps because he was content with his day's catch. He was feeling unusually talkative.

'Do you want to understand the secrets of fishing?' he asked me, in his usual abrupt manner, which was rough rather than rude. He continued his monologue without waiting for a reply; he knew I was always eager for any scraps of knowledge or information.

'The secret of fishing is to treat the fish as an extension of one's own mind,' he said. It sounded wise and profound, and I considered it in the context of the enigmatic stranger who had invaded my life.

'Life is a river,' he continued, 'and all life is embodied in this river, this Ganga that flows through our lives. Bhavishya gyana da, bhoot gyana da, vartaman gyana da, she carries in her the secrets of the future, the past, and the ever-flowing present.'

I looked at the river, the mighty goddess. In a day her anger was gone, and she was playful now, a loving, forgiving, easy-going river on a late spring afternoon. As summer approached, the water would mysteriously become colder, and I could then sit for hours on a rock by the shore with my feet negotiating the icy motion of the swift young waves.

'If life is a river we must be the fish,' I said, more to keep the conversation going than out of any philosophical interest.

'You missed the whole point, Shakuntala,' he said resignedly, shaking his head. 'The fish are the river, as the river is the fish.' It was getting too complicated for me, I didn't care whether I was the river or the fish, I was hungry and impatiently surveyed Kundan's catch. I was not a shakahari like my brother Guresvara. My mother ate no meat or fish, but Srijan's household did not abide by any such rules. Lighting a three-twig fire there by the beach, not a household fire but a quick fire of nomads, we seasoned his catch with salt and turmeric and ate it heartily. We left the bones and other remains behind the rocks for the river crabs to devour, or the crows if they got there first.

I was brooding about the woman again. I still did not know her name. Just the thought of her made me ache from the inside. It was as though my heart had collapsed, and my blood was rotting like stagnant water. I wondered what she was doing at this moment. Perhaps Srijan was tired; he might have asked her to fan him in our bedchamber. Surely it was still too cool to need a fan? She might be pressing his feet, then, as handmaidens do, or even massaging his high forehead.

I felt flushed and angry. As I got to my feet to leave, the fisherman gave me a knowing look. 'Remember, you have to become the fish to catch it,' he said, before lapsing into his usual mournful silence. I hurried back to the house, full of purpose, determined to retrieve my life from the intruder.

Srijan was not at home. The woman too was nowhere to be seen. My husband was a busy man, an important man, with constant business in the neighbouring villages. I did not expect him to stay at home like a woman. But this handmaiden, she had no reason not to be awaiting me!

It was a while before she appeared. Her upper lip was covered with a thin film of sweat, and she looked excited and happy. Then she saw me and recomposed her face into an expression of strained calm. When her face was still, it did not fade into repose; it merely suspended its animation and became a mask, a blank, inscrutable screen I could not penetrate.

I examined her features in silence. Her eyebrows were curved like a strung bow. Her large, cold eyes, framed by thick upturned lashes, could be described as almond-shaped or like the fish that lurked in the waters of the Ganga, depending on which poetic style one preferred. Her nose was long but slim, and two glittering nose rings adorned the perfectly shaped curve of her nostrils. Her lips were large and sensuous, her neck a proud column. She was like a high-spirited stallion, or an unfolding lotus bud. I had always considered myself beautiful, until the day I met her. Now I felt like an overgrown child or a gawky village woman.

'What is your name?' I asked her, for this was something I needed to know but had been too proud to ask. 'And where is it that you come from?'

'My name is Kamalini,' she replied melodiously. 'I come from the lands of the east, near Lichhavi, from the village of Nandankot, where my father was the headman.'

A mere headman's daughter and such exalted airs!

'We have a republic, we follow no kings, we bow before no emperor. And my father, he is a very learned man,' she continued, as though reading my thoughts.

'So, Kamalini, don't you miss your home? Don't you wish you were back with your learned father?' I asked, summoning all the sarcasm at my command.

Her eyes met mine. They carried no expression but

contempt. 'My father does not want me back in Nandankot,' she said tonelessly. 'Is there something I can do for you?'

'Sit down here beside me, Kamalini,' I said ingratiatingly. The fisherman had to be one with the fish. 'Will you help me do up my hair, Kamalini? I want to braid it like yours. You have such beautiful hair!'

She knelt down behind me. I felt her deft, firm fingers on my scalp, patiently untangling the windblown mess. The fine-toothed ivory comb had never been put to more rigorous use. My meagre tresses were pulled back tightly into neat double-braids, and then put up in two coils, with long ivory hairpins to hold them up. 'Don't look in the mirror yet,' she said sternly, running out into the garden, for once abandoning her perfect poise. She returned with a handful of dhatri flowers, which she inserted deftly into the braid, dangling the last bunch behind my left ear. The blossoms made the room fragrant as a bower, and when at last I looked into the burnished mirror-plate I was pleased with what I saw.

Kamalini was suddenly formal again. 'May I leave now?' she asked, in the same toneless voice that bordered always on the insolent.

I thanked her profusely, some of the pent-up hostility and anger that had been simmering inside me temporarily suspended. I am not proficient at hating, and in a strange way I admired Kamalini.

Srijan was quick to notice my new hairstyle that night. 'You are so beautiful, Shakuntala,' he murmured. 'I have never seen you look better.' I said nothing, I was not going to rise to the bait of Kamalini's goodwill so easily.

It was the night of the new moon. We embraced through the dark hours as we used to before, our love-making more urgent with the faintly narcotic smell of the flowers in my hair. I was floating in a very real rapture; it reminded me of the Soma wine I had drunk during the Agnicayana rituals, and of the flickering light in the hidden shrine of the temple where freshly plucked flowers adorned the stone yoni. There was an edge to our passion. The old trust had been replaced by a more demanding need. With Srijan I had few inhibitions, but that night I came close to losing all shame; I came close to being what I later became, with another. When Srijan entered me it was different from how it had been, he took me in ways he had never done before. I would be lying if I were to say that I did not enjoy it. The hurt and anger that had been raging inside had transformed me. At the height of our union, as Srijan spilled his seed into my womb, I was thinking not of him or of myself, but of a tall, large-boned woman with scornful eyes.

7

The days passed uneasily, in suppressed silence. Srijan rarely spoke to Kamalini. When he did, it was to express a wish or command. As for me, I was determined to befriend this mysterious dasi, my handmaiden, hate her as I might in the privacy of my heart. I would instruct her to massage me with sandal oil. When I felt her knowing, sensuous touch on my flesh, I would suffer paroxysms of jealousy. Who was she, why had Srijan brought her into our household?

It was around this time that my brother stopped on his way to the high mountains to visit us. Guresvara was a scholar and a mendicant, he could think and dream and roam the world with the abandon of a wandering cloud. He was like me, and yet my complete opposite. I was a woman, it was my lot to please my husband, to live at his pleasure. Guresvara was his own master. But, although he did not know it, a bit of me travelled with him wherever he went. As a flea travels on a dog, or pollen on a bee, so my mind travelled with my brother.

Despite their considerable difference in age, Guresvara and Srijan were friends. They liked and respected each other. I felt secure in their company, and for a while I became part of the larger, busier world to which I wanted so desperately to belong. Kamalini lay outside and beyond this circle. Guresvara was my brother and she could not break into the shared bond of our togetherness.

My brother was looking thinner than ever before. The rigorous fasting and penitence of his calling had left him gaunt and pale. The prominent new lines upon his emaciated cheeks made him appear almost a stranger. I bent low to touch his feet when he arrived. He greeted me with the decorum proper to a renunciate meeting a householder, for bonds of blood hold little meaning to those who have forsaken the transient relationships of this world.

'You look well, sister,' he said, his joy at our reunion lighting his face, playing unexpected tricks on its stern set. For a while I saw another face before me, glimpsed the petulant boy who wanted sometimes to play rather than listen to the edicts and sutras and the endless pontificating of his tutor. The moment passed swiftly.

Since Guresvara was a famous Sanyasi, all the members of our household, and even visitors from distant homesteads, came to see him and obtain his blessings. Guresvara dealt with them with his customary good humour, and they departed content in the sunshine of his love and understanding that seemed to envelop each one separately.

Guresvara was always courteous. He had a slow, measured

manner, and never found fault with anyone. He neither mocked nor criticized, for in his eyes everyone and everything was a reflection of the godhead. He was noble beyond belief, as of course he could afford to be, with only god and himself to worry about, and they being the same in his philosophy. Sometimes I would get irritated by his goodness, his humility, his unremitting courtesy, for in an inexplicable way all these qualities added up to nothing but a great arrogance. He believed only in what he called the 'sword-edge of discrimination' and he succeeded in making me feel selfish and stupid.

Kamalini too wanted to meet Guresvara. Of course I could not stop her. My brother, who always thought well of everyone, never for a moment questioned or doubted her presence in my household. He examined her intently and asked her where she had come from. 'I have been to the land of the Lichhavis in my travels,' he said when she told him, his eyes taking in every detail of her clothes and appearance. 'Do you not feel lonely, sister, so far from your home?'

Kamalini looked him straight in the eye. There was no contempt in her face now, it was not impassive and mask-like. She looked nervous and her lips were tremulous, as though she were about to break down and start weeping. 'This is my home now,' she said, her proud head cast down. She was for once behaving in a manner befitting a dasi. I enjoyed her discomfiture. She looked like a cat that has been drenched in a bucket of water. Still I was not moved to feel sorry for her.

My brother asked Kamalini to seat herself on the rush mat laid out for visitors. 'What is your religion, sister?' he asked.

She had recomposed herself. 'None,' she replied, with a defiant toss of her head. 'I believe in no one and nothing.' The cat was dry again.

'What was the religion of your father?' Guresvara persisted.

'It is a matter of no consequence,' she said, her eyes focussed somewhere high above Guresvara's head. I found myself admiring her spirit. It was difficult for a woman to talk thus to a man, especially a man as holy and good as my brother.

Guresvara nodded abstractedly and began talking to another visitor, an elder of a distant village whose family we had both known since we were young. My brother's robes were dyed the deep ochre of a mendicant's clothes. His feet were callused from years of constant walking. His head was shaven except for the tuft of his bundled up topknot. The afternoon sun streamed in from the west, and cast an effulgence around him, a halo of saffron and gold. I felt cleansed of my doubts and fears. There was nothing sordid or suspicious about Kamalini's presence, nothing to question in her strange arrival. Kamalini herself had softened, some of the sullen, silent anger had been leeched out of her and she seemed less hostile. But the feeling did not last. A mere toss of her perfectly shaped head, and I was not so forgiving any more. The manner in which she turned to look through the door at the garden outside, with effortless, animal pride, like a panther, filled me with blind anger.

The sloping garden that fronted the house yielded a constant profusion of flowering madhavi, malti and mimosa. The flowers, that was what she was looking at. She coveted them. It was juvenile to resent this, but I did. This was *my* garden; I was the mistress of everything in it.

There was an old man labouring up to the house. As his bent frame emerged from the incline of the hill, he began plucking the flowers. He hobbled in carrying a handful of my precious buds, which he offered reverentially to my brother.

'What fragrant blossoms,' Guresvara said, in his usual kindly manner.

I exploded with anger. 'Beautiful indeed!' I exclaimed. 'And plucked from the carefully tended garden of your host!'

Srijan stared at me in surprise. My brother was, as ever, slow to react. 'What fragrant flowers,' he murmured again, seating the old man down before blessing him.

'Such possessiveness is unbecoming in you, Shakuntala,' he remonstrated, after the thief had departed. But the real thief was among us, looking at me with the amused pity of a victor. 'Flowers are like human beings,' my brother went on. 'They belong only to the soil in which they are reared. Kings, wise men and good wives should learn this lesson well.'

'Women, especially good wives, are ever transplanted from the homes in which they are reared, and then new plants and creepers take root in their soil!' I retorted. I was tired of his magnanimity. Did he not see my situation? Could he not sense my pain?

But Guresvara knew how to handle people and situations. He did not engage with me in debate. 'Will you entertain us with a song, O lady of Lichhavi,' he said, addressing himself to my enemy. 'Sing us something that will make you and all of us feel happy.'

Kamalini looked quite amazed by his request, but she agreed without any protestations. The music of our mountains is either merry or mournful, and sometimes it is both, but Kamalini's song was sung in a different voice and tone altogether. It was high-pitched and sweet, full of the most unexpected trills and extravagances. My brother seemed transported to another world. His head was set at a strange angle, frozen halfway to a nod, as though he were trying to locate something he could not hear, find some hidden note in the music. Srijan looked blank, studiously withholding his reaction. I wondered if he had heard her sing before, during that long journey they made together from the lands of the east, from her village Nandankot, to this house here in the mountains.

That night, Guresvara and Srijan sat up until late, talking about the changes that were sweeping the land. The nations of the east were in turmoil, Guresvara said. The religion of the Sakyamuni, Gautama Buddha, was destroying the foundations of the old faith. The Aryan religion, the Vedic path of the Triyodharma, was under assault from the Pashanda cults, from the Sakyas, the Ajivikas, and all those who did not properly honour the pitras, the spirits of the ancestors.

Srijan was politely silent through Guresvara's lamentations. His mother had taken the vows of a Sakya nun before she died, and he professed whatever faith, Brahminical or Buddhist, that was convenient, expedient or honourable in the circumstances. After my brother had spoken of the dangers to the true faith, Srijan tactfully questioned him on details of his travels. This was, I suspected, more for reasons of trade and commerce than out of any religious or spiritual curiosity.

Guresvara talked of his journey to the lands of the Madhya Desha, the middle kingdoms, where the Narmada flowed through canyons of marble rock. He told us of copper and gold mines where men burrowed deep into the entrails of the earth to extract precious metals. He had encountered a Khan-adhyaksha, in charge of the mines, and a Loha-adhyaksha, the officer in charge of processing metals, who were brothers. These brothers were also alchemists, and they were convinced that they had at last discovered the secrets of the parasmani, the philosopher's stone that could turn base metals to gold.

Of course, Guresvara had to add something philosophical to the story, predictably about the inner self being of gold and the world only dross metal, as also how the parasmani of true discrimination could get us through the travails of life, and so on.

Sometimes I felt that my brother, for all his wisdom, knew much less about real life than I did. He was the sequestered one, not me, for although he had travelled the world, as I had not, he chose to see only what he wanted to.

My husband listened to these stories of alchemists and the elusive parasmani, but he was a practical man, and was more interested in gathering information regarding the new fabrics and textiles being manufactured in the great cities of the plains. Factories, or sutrashalas, were being set up for the spinning of yarn and karmantas commissioned for the specialized manufacture of fabrics woven of this yarn. Rolls of expensive, shimmering Cheenapatti silk arrived every day from the trade routes of the north, from the Hara Huraka, the land of the Huns, and Cheena-bhumi, the country beyond the high mountains. Srijan wanted to assess the effects of these new weaves and fabrics on the market for traditional silks, which constituted such an important part of his trade.

Although I liked the rich silks, of which I had several in my wooden dower case, there was nothing I enjoyed wearing more than the soft flax woven by the village women in our hills. Silks and new, intricate weaves were not the reason why I listened intently to their conversation. It was the picture of the bigger world their words conjured up that left me breathless with excitement. A world of limitless possibilities, awaiting discovery.

I sighed loudly. My emotions were compounded of impatience and longing. My brother and my husband both heard the sigh, and separately misunderstood the meaning behind it. Guresvara thought I was grieving for his departure, and consoled me, in his gentle manner, telling me that he had now shed all mortal ties, so I was not to sorrow at his leaving. 'All women in this world are my sisters and my mothers, but

you, more than any other, are still the dearest, Shakuntala,'
he said. Though his declaration did not move me, I composed
my face to look suitably serious.

Srijan was silent, but I could read the expression in his
face. He thought I was grieving because I had not yet
conceived a child. Men, although they rule and direct the
world, can lack perception in a way that is sometimes
alarming to their mothers and sisters. But I could not tell
them the truth, I could not talk of my impatience to see the
world, it would have been unseemly and inappropriate.

So I changed the subject and asked Guresvara about the
abandoned Matrika shrine, the temple of the goddess where
I had spent that strange, wonderful night. I couched my
question cleverly, for I did not feel ready to share those
memories. Never having kept any secrets from Srijan, I had
to tread cautiously.

'The seven goddesses are the consorts of the gods,'
Guresvara explained. 'The Sapta Matrikas—Brahmani,
Maheshwari, Kaumari, Vaishnavi, Varahi, Indrani and
Narsimhi—are the feminine energies that activate our world.
When joined by a male energy, they make for harmony and
stability. After all, we are all children of the Eternal Mother.'
He looked pious and complacent, and I wondered once again
whether I really loved or admired my sanctimonious brother.

'Then why is the temple abandoned?' I persisted. 'Why
are there no idols, no priest? Where did they all go? What
happened to them?'

Guresvara coughed self-importantly. 'The Vastu Shastras

tell us, dear sister, that there is no site in the whole world more unpropitious than an abandoned temple. What I am about to tell you is not for women to know, but a learned man must answer all sincere questions in the same spirit. This temple was once famed for having the true voice of the goddess speak from it. If any woman asked a question there, it was answered, in human voice. Being the reply of a goddess, it was necessarily true. But truth of the differentiated kind has many gradations, and what the goddess spoke was not possibly the only truth, or the best truth to be told.'

Outside, the moon gleamed behind the fig and mulberry trees, where the birds of the night, inauspicious birds, sat awake and listening. They, too, heard the question I put to my learned brother: 'What happened to this truth?' I was thinking of the rock-demoness I had met years ago—in dream or reality, I couldn't be sure—and the Agnicayana ritual, and the priests from Kashi with their worries about my defilement.

'The question of truth has to be constantly addressed according to the changing temper of the times,' my brother replied. 'A great sage once came to these hills in the course of his travels. He slept the night near the temple and listened to the goddess-speak. He did not like what he heard, and so he had the temple boarded up. He recited some secret sutras and commanded the goddess to be silent. Shakti without Shiva is not feasible, he declared. The men of the village were with him in his enterprise, for they too did not like the voice of the goddess. They said it made their women too assertive; it led to disorder, and disorder, you understand, sister, is never the true state. And then, one day, the sage left as well. It was time for him to continue with his travels. Whatever remains of the temple, remains. Who knows, the Matrika may one day choose to return to her temple—the vermilion-anointed goddess, she of the many faces. It is not easy to forget one's mother . . .'

Surely Shiva needed Shakti as Shakti needed Shiva? Women's blood, women's wombs, why did the priests fear them so much? I did not voice these thoughts. Guresvara looked sad, like the vulnerable brother I had once known, and sometimes loved. Behind his pose of high detachment, he had cared deeply for our mother. Despite his self-assurance and his saffron robes, I knew that he was missing her now.

It was dawn, and a holy man does not spend more than a night in a householder's dwellings. It was time for Guresvara to resume his travels. Touching his feet, I sought his blessings before he left, and presented him with an offering of woollen robes dyed ochre, which I had kept ready for a year, awaiting this visit. There were also flowers, and some fruit, a few silver-minted coins discreetly knotted up in a scrap of silk, and local red rice to remind him of the home he had left behind. As he was about to step out, my brother turned back from the threshold. This was completely uncharacteristic of his unfaltering nature. He looked at me searchingly, something close to concern in his eyes. 'Is there any kumkum in the house, Shakuntala?' he asked. I brought out the carved box, heaped with the auspicious vermilion powder I used to adorn my forehead. 'I want you to anoint my brow,' he said, 'to remind me of the Mother.' Deeply moved by his request, I did as Guresvara asked. In spite of his great learning, he remained in so many ways a little boy. I had held him and soothed away his fears of the dark—it was all too far in the past now. We could both have loved each other better.

Guresvara's scant possessions were tied into a modest cloth bundle, which was in turn attached to the wooden staff that doubled as his walking stick. In his other hand he held the kamandalu, in which he sought alms, and the trident, sacred to Shiva. Carefully unbundling the cloth packet, Guresvara extracted a matted brown object I did not recognize. 'Here is a coconut from the lands of the west,' he said. 'It confers fertility and abundance. Dear sister, it will bless you with all you want and desire.' He strode out into the darkness, which carried only the promise of morning, leaving me with my husband Srijan, my lord, master and dearest friend.

Although I was tired from not having slept all night, I was delighted by my brother's parting gift. I had never before seen a whole coconut, only the dried and desiccated shards that sometimes made their way so far to the north. Srijan watched me quietly. We were both sad that Guresvara had left. It was as though his going foreboded other departures.

I went to the edge of our sloping garden to see my brother stride down the incline to the bottom of the hill. Srijan came up behind me. 'Don't fly away, my shakun bird!' he said, stroking my tangled hair, which I had left loose in defiance of Kamalini's ministrations. I felt happy and excited at the idea, and flapped my arms as though suspended in flight. This made my husband smile, and we got down to laughter and kissing. We were too tired to do anything more, and fell asleep even though it was already morning. When at last I awoke, late in the mid-afternoon, I felt as buoyant and happy as I had been after the Agnicayana ritual, before Srijan had set off on that fateful journey.

The thing about happiness is that one never recognizes it until long after the moment has passed. I loved Srijan more than anyone I have ever loved. He was like a father, a mother, a brother, a sister, a lover, a friend; he was more to me than myself. I can feel this now, when it is far too late to do anything about it, but it is not as though I did not know it even then.

8

 Kamalini was behaving extremely strangely. She would be sullen for days on end, then suddenly become excessively sweet and helpful. One morning I caught her examining herself in the mirror in my room, a spiteful, unpleasant smile spread across her face. Mostly I found her in shadows and corners, never too far from me, silent as a ghost.

I did not know what to do with her. I did not need a handmaiden. I was not a child, I could look after myself. As for the household, it had run perfectly even before I was married, and would continue to do so; I wasn't required to do anything. I was not a grand lady either, or a princess living in a palace. I was simply Shakuntala of the low mountains, Shakuntala of the unbraided hair, of the flaxen garments. No, I did not need a dasi.

I tried to make friends with Kamalini, but it was difficult, given her strange disposition. I am not a particularly clever woman, but I could see that she disliked, even despised me.

Every time she massaged my body with fragrant oil or braided my hair into an elaborate style, her clever probing fingers seemed like hostile inquisitors. She was eager to know all my secrets, to judge and assess me as though on a battlefield. She made me feel uneasy and uncomfortable in my own house and it was no wonder that, try as I might, I could not get to like her.

Srijan made a visit to the neighbouring villages. He decided not to walk there, and travelled in the uncomfortable palanquin used for longer journeys. When he returned, he was limping and his feet were swollen and dusty. One of the palanquin-bearers had fallen ill, and so Srijan had had to trudge back for most of the way. I was once again suffering the hated monthly curse of the ritu. From the confines of the women's room I instructed the maid Dhania to remove his boar-skin sandals and wash his feet with milk and water. Incarcerated in that dark, airless hole, I could overhear Kamalini talking to my husband. 'May I press your feet, master?' she asked, in a seemingly modest and courteous way. Yet my wary ears could detect a seductive undertone in her voice. Srijan's reply could not be heard, but he sounded distracted and preoccupied. I spent the night weeping, wondering what it was that the lady from Lichhavi was doing in our bedchamber.

When the time of my ritu had passed, after I bathed and underwent the ritual purification, I lay on our marital bed with Srijan and asked him how he had enjoyed Kamalini's ministrations. 'She pressed my feet,' he replied. 'She is a submissive and conscientious dasi. We are lucky to have her with us.'

I turned away from him. A papiha was sheltering by the windowsill singing its insistent love song. 'Pee-kahan?' it asked. 'Pee-kahan?

'Pee-kahan?' Srijan mimicked, taking me into the warm comfort of his arms. I listened to the pounding of his heart, inhaled his familiar body smells, of sandal oil and the sweet fragrance of earth. But the unmistakable, elusive scent of musk also clung to him, strange, unthinkable, an animal scent.

The next morning I discovered a crow feather under my pillow. It could not have flown there on its own. There was also a bowl of honeyed figs in my room. When I ate one I felt inexplicably dizzy, and continued to do so for a few days. I had the fruit removed. Kamalini brought in another bowl, and asked me in her usual inscrutable way if there was any reason why I had thrown the figs away. Often I would find stones in the food served to me, lodged in the cooked gruel or the lentils. Then I found a dead cat in the garden. These were strange happenings, disturbing omens.

The dead cat unsettled me the most. It had been dismembered, its insides exposed to the elements. I looked at it with morbid fascination. It was difficult to believe that this cat, a supple black shadow which stole milk from the kitchen (or so Dhania maintained) was now no longer capable of will or movement. It struck me with startling clarity that I too would die, Srijan would too, we would all one day leave this world and move on to the ones beyond. The thought filled me with unease.

I wanted to talk about this, to understand. I carried little faith in the village priest and his stories about the path of the soul after death, of the various levels of purgatory, of the pitralok and the heaven of Indra and so on. How, after all, could anybody who had not actually died know these things? I decided to ask my friend, the fisherman. He was never muddled by words and appearances, he knew things in a more basic way. I could believe what he told me.

'What is death?' I asked Kundan. He was sitting, bent over, at his favourite spot by the edge of the sand bank, where the two black rocks he called the lovers jutted out of the waves. There was a fishing line in the water, but he was not holding the rod, which had been left to stand, propped up by an improvised bamboo-hold.

'You see, my learned Shakuntala, there is an element in which each of us survives, in which we can thrive. This fish, for instance, which is so happy in the water, which swims about without a care in the depths of the holy river, once this fish is out of its true element, released into the air that you and I can so easily breathe, it dies.' He matched his actions to his words, and a giant fish flew out of the water with a swishing sound to land on the line at my feet. It was flapping about tiredly, engaged in a defeated death-dance.

'That is Death. It is the loss of our natural environment. If this fish could suddenly learn to breathe in air, it would continue to live, it could have an afterlife. There are creatures that can lead such double lives, such as the frogs that crowd into your house during the rainy weather,' as indeed they did, and never failed to frighten me . . . 'and there are beings who can do the same, who continue to live on after they die, because they are not dependent on their bodies alone. As the frogs can live by your doorstep or in the village pond with equal ease, so these beings straddle both the worlds of the dead and the undead.'

His explanation did not satisfy me. It seemed logical and incontrovertible, it was not frightening, yet it sounded like prattle to me. Disappointed, I rose to leave. I took one last look at the enormous fish that lay by my feet. It was now finally dead. It was as ready to be eaten as I was ready to eat it.

Back in the house, Kamalini had prepared special sweets made of jaggery and sesame for me. 'These will help you conceive,' she said. 'My mother taught me how to make them in our village in Nandankot.'

'Well then, why don't you use them for that purpose yourself?' I asked sharply. 'I am sure you would be as glad to conceive as I would, my lady of Lichhavi! Wouldn't you like to have a child, a handsome boy?'

'I already have a child, a handsome young boy,' she replied with downcast eyes, her face like a despondent thundercloud that is about to burst into rain. 'I left him behind in Nandankot.'

My mind filled up with dread and rage. Whose child was it? Who was Kamalini, this woman who smelt of musk and roses, her body taut like a strung bow? What was her relationship with my husband? All the old questions began torturing me with renewed vigour.

'Why have you left your son behind? What are you doing so far away from your home?' I was breathless with fear as I asked the question; it felt as though an enormous chasm had opened up at my feet, a sheer rock cliff that separated my question and her answer.

'I cannot tell you the reasons,' she said, neither nervous nor agitated. 'You can, if you wish, ask this question of your husband Srijan, my most honoured master. This is my home now, and my son is happy and well looked after where he is.'

I was falling down the deep chasm. My voice shook as I made up some inconsequential remark to cover up my confusion. I walked out into the garden. The afternoon sun blinded me. My eyes brimmed with unshed tears. I could not believe that this was happening to me. The smell of sandalwood and earth knew the scent of musk and roses. The world was a place of treason, not of trust.

The learned say that we have a gross body and a subtle body. My subtle body had collapsed into my gross body. I was made of stone, every one of my senses weighted down with anguish. I could neither confront nor address this pain. The only sanctuary I knew was the temple, but I did not want to go there. I remembered the day of the Agnicayana ritual, when my husband had worn the golden breastplate, draped the antelope skin around his shoulders. We had drunk Soma juice together, it had been a time of fulfilment. It was over now; I was no longer the same person, every breath I took established that I was someone else.

I lay down on my bed, first ensuring there were no crow feathers hidden under the pillow of soft semul seeds. I could hear my heartbeat, the sound of my head pounding. It was not so, my suspicions could not be true. Srijan was a wise man, a patient man. He loved me. No child of his would be born of another woman. I must trust him.

I called for Kamalini. I had her braid my hair and decorate it with mogra flowers. I instructed her to anoint my body with perfumed oils. Then I put anjana in my eyes and alta on my feet, and awaited Srijan's entry into our bedchamber. That night our love-making was different from how it had been for some months. Srijan seemed surprised by my ardour and reluctant to respond to it, but I was possessed. I was no longer Shakuntala, the wife of Srijan, his friend and confidante. I became Kamalini. As we glided and moved in each other, my closed eyes and panting body belonged not to me but to her. Srijan seemed sad. He was, as ever, a considerate, providing lover, but there was no joy or abandon in his movements, and his eyes were observing me carefully.

As the moment of fulfilment approached, Srijan withdrew from within me. 'I am sorry, Shakuntala,' he said. 'Forgive me, perhaps I am not quite well today.'

Every evening I darkened my eyes, anointed myself with scented oil. Kamalini would apply a paste of sandalwood beneath my breasts, perfume my hair with incense fumes and comb and braid it. I would both swoon and recoil at her confident, knowing touch. Obsessed by our night-games, I set about seducing my husband, shuddering and moaning like a harlot, writhing and turning. My yoni was the one part of my body which was still alive, all pain, joy and hope concentrated in that one orifice. The rest of me was insulated and deadened by hurt, but there I was hungry and supple. I wanted desperately to kindle my husband's body, steal his strength, own and possess power over him. But I could not succeed. Our love had vanished.

My rival had virtually disappeared from my life. She had made herself invisible. Her eyes never met mine. When she talked to me, she looked only at my feet. One evening, as I was walking by the river, I heard the distant sound of a woman humming a mournful song. I knew it was Kamalini, though I could have sworn the voice came from the other side of the river. When I went back home, she was seated outside my chamber, silent, head bowed, though her spine was erect.

In the mornings, my mind would be swept by wild fancies. Perhaps I too could become a monk or a renunciate. Our religion had no place for women, but the Buddhist orders inducted women as novices. Like Srijan's mother, I would sport a shaved head and wear ochre robes to live a life of penitence. I would walk and travel and see the world. My brother and I would engage in learned conversation. I had heard of the great public debates where sages like the Shankaracharya argued over matters of philosophy and logic. The participants were garlanded with freshly plucked flowers, and whosoever it was whose garland wilted first acknowledged the victory of the other. In my daydreams I pictured Guresvara, defeated and dispirited, dead flowers drooping around his bowed neck, while I smiled at him, wreathed in lotus buds, gracious in victory.

I did not practically understand how to go about becoming a Buddhist nun. 'Arise! Commence a new life!' the Bhikkuni had said. How did one do that? The nearest monastery was a day's walk away, but I did not know the direction in which it lay. I could not ask the village priest, for he belonged to the established dharma, and would only discourage a defection . . .

And then I would dismiss the whole idea, for becoming a nun would clearly be conceding defeat to Kamalini.

At night the hungers awakened again. I sought only to arouse my husband's desire, to conquer him with the wildest caresses. I could see the moon from my window; Raka, the accomplice of lovers and madmen. A woman imbedded with seed in the period of the waxing moon was more likely to bear a child. Every night, as I dressed for the bedchamber, anointing my underparts with unguents and fragrant oils, I prayed to Siniwali, the moon-goddess who aids conception and gifts life to the wombs of women: 'O Siniwali, set the germ, set the seed . . . that in the tenth month I may bear the image of Thy Divinity!'

Dhania had warned me of evil spirits and ghouls who attacked expectant mothers. She had cautioned me to beware particularly of Arayi, the ever-screeching she-fiend, one-eyed and limping, destroyer of unborn seed. I took her advice now and watered the sacred tulsi plant in the courtyard every morning and evening to keep Arayi at bay. Yet I failed to conceive. As I sat on the floor in the women's room, the straw matting permeated by the smell of stale blood, I was more deeply defeated than I had ever been before. There was no way out in sight. I was doomed to be barren.

Through those months I sought solace in the rhythm of the cowsheds. The cows had kind eyes, and were content to be tethered to a post and have their milk stolen from them twice a day. They knew how to give of their abundance, how to share. I too could learn from them, I who had teats that gave no milk, whose udders had no calves to comfort.

I rose early to feed the cows, mixing old grass with the new. I brought them water, and saw that the floor of their stalls was dry and clean. They rewarded me with a knowing moo as they nuzzled on the hay. When the woman helping me had left, I stayed back, sitting on a log stool by the door, sometimes for several hours. The smells of the cowshed reminded me of my sad, hard mother, whom I now missed with surprising intensity. Sometimes I hummed a prayer from the Rig Veda which she had taught me. It was dedicated to Aranyani, the goddess of the wilderness:

> Lady of the forest, goddess of the wild, who seeks not the
> villages!
> Here is one calling to his cow, another there hath felled a
> tree:

At evening time the traveller in the woods fancies he hears
a scream.
Know this, the goddess never slays unless some murderous
enemy approaches.
Man eats his fill of ripened fruit and then takes, even as he
walks, the rest!
Praise the mother of all sylvan things
Who tills, but hoards not her sacred store of food!

It was a simple, straightforward verse of even metre, not
obscure like the hymns to the great gods. As I hummed, the
song became one with the tinkle of cowbells, the rustle of
leaves in the drowsy trees, and the chirrup of the vrsrava, the
friendly forest-cricket. It soothed and comforted me, and late
one afternoon, my heart lighter after I had finished the song,
I decided to walk through the forest to the abandoned
temple. I did not want the sight of Kamalini to sour my
mood.

I stroked the cows before leaving. A white cow called
Dasyu was the most bountiful of all our cattle. She had
become a particular favourite of mine. Dasyu had what can
only be described as a pious face, and looked like a noble
matron of a well-born family. She had calved recently, and
the heifer was spotted with black. 'Goodbye, mother,' I
whispered, patting her fondly before barring the door. She
flicked her tail in response, as though to bid me farewell.

It was late in the month of Chaitra. The forest trees were
bursting with blossom. Laburnums blazed against a sharp blue
sky. Sheets of bakul flowers lay scattered at my feet. The

summer would be upon us soon, but at the moment the grass glowed with the peculiar verdant green of late spring. The smell of earth reminded me of Srijan's skin, so I lay down and breathed deeply of the fragrance of the soil. An eagle was circling above. A mountain bird broke the air in gentle swoops and dives. I had climbed high up the hill. The almost vertical slope was covered with trees and vines and creepers. The Ganga, far below me, was a shining rope of silver.

I imagined the course of the great river as it flowed through our hills to the lands below, to the cities and towns and settlements where my brother Guresvara and my husband Srijan had travelled. I had heard that there were dolphins in the waters downriver, and mermaids who seduced travellers and robbed them of their memories of home. There were crocodiles whose bellies were filled with the gold and jewels of the humans they had devoured. Srijan had told me of Pataliputra, with its wooden barricades and famed scholars and courtesans. I knew of Ujjaini, the holy city on the banks of the Narmada where Kalidasa had lived, dreaming up his Shakuntala. And I knew of that incomparable city, golden Kashi, timeless and undying, where even sinners and lost souls could find redemption. I wished I were a river, to flow where I pleased, to wash the world with my waters.

My face buried in the grass, I observed a line of ants approaching in military formation. They were headed towards their mud fortress on the path to the temple. Anthills are like cities, too, and the ancient masters of the Vastu Shastras, the builders of great cities, had learnt much from them. I had gathered that cities were crowded places. I was certain that the nagariks who lived there were different from the kind of people I met every day, people who lacked even the most common manners. The nagariks were rich and resplendent, and always in a hurry. They moved around in horse-cars and chariots, and they certainly did not gawk at elephants.

I spent much of the day wandering in the forest. By the time I finally reached the temple, the day was already waning. The sunlight held a mellow transience, like a guest who is about to leave. I was surprised to see an ancient crone in ragged clothes sitting on the temple steps. I approached her with caution, for who does not know of the malicious spirits that reside in the woods and prey on the bodies of trusting men and women? Climbing up, I noticed her feet first. They were indescribably dirty, and old and abused like the worn stone steps on which she was perched. Her toes were clawed and crooked, their broken skin the colour of slate. She seemed extraordinarily pleased to see me, for some reason. Wheezing and snorting to indicate her approval, she smiled at me, an old woman's smile, simple, wide, and jagged for all the missing and broken teeth. I summoned the courage to smile back. She dug her hands into the folds of her skirt, as though searching for something. At last she discovered a withered amalaka, a sour gooseberry, which she offered me with a shy grimace. Her hands were worse than her feet, cracked and grimy, the nails coated with filth, yet I accepted her gift, and put it away in the delicately embroidered pouch attached to my antariya.

It was quiet and peaceful in the temple. I peered into the hidden chamber. Flowers and fruit were strewn around the yoni, and the young wick of the oil lamp testified that it had only recently been lit. The old woman followed me in. Was she the unlikely, mysterious custodian of the temple? I turned around, but although I wanted very much to talk to her, I was not sure how I should address her.

Her rheumy eyes searched mine. 'I know you, daughter,' she said.

'But I don't know you, mother,' I responded, for in all honesty I had never seen her before.

She continued to stare at me. 'You might have to spend the night here again. I cannot stay, but you will be safe.' She spoke well, like a learned high-born person, not a common village woman. She threw me another smile and began walking away. I came out of the inner chamber to watch the stooped figure go down the steps with some effort and walk into the woods. A new moon hung in the sky, a tusk of light against the dark. It was already too late for me to return home.

I settled down on the steps where the old woman had sat before me. What would I be like when I was her age, when my hair was moon-white and my spine bent? Would I have sons and daughters to carry on our line? Would the sons be good to me, would their wives cherish me? Would I, dreaded thought, have to take myself to the forest, condemn myself to the life of a lonely old crone because my lord and master Srijan had taken on new and younger wives? The Manava

Dharma Shastra says: 'A barren wife should be abandoned in the tenth year, one who bears only daughters in the twelfth, and one whose children all die in the fifteenth.' I did not allow myself to think of Kamalini. She was a mere dasi. Even if my husband chose to consort with her, she could not threaten me. So I told myself, but in my heart I felt hollow and afraid.

Night had settled in the woods. The forest sounds were getting louder. I was apprehensive about being away from home. Srijan would be annoyed by my disappearance, it would only further the distance between us. What would I say to him tomorrow—the old lie, that I had slept on a tree because I was afraid of bears? He would not believe me. I was debating telling him the truth and wondering where that would lead, when I saw a light spring up in the dark and move through the forest, approaching the temple. Caution and good sense led me to withdraw to the secret chamber where the oil lamp flickered. I crept in, crouching low on the floor so that I could stay hidden and watch out for whoever or whatever was approaching.

It was my husband. He was alone, and held a torch in his hand. He had come in search of me. Two men from the neighbouring village followed in his trail, some distance away.

I was racked by alternating waves of joy and panic. 'I am here, Srijan, my lord,' I whispered, extricating myself from behind the stone wall. The light of the torch lit up his face. It was impassive, but it was not angry.

'You may go, honoured friends. I am grateful for your help,' he said to the villagers, who were rough and rustic and in a hurry to return home. Srijan took the torch in his hand and dug it into the ground outside the temple. It slithered and danced in the wind, looking joyous and celebratory, for fire and night both oppose and support each other. We stood together in the dark. The stars shimmered in the sky. The night breeze was cool but not cold. Crows cawed in concert in the forest, in an intense argument, or a crow conclave. We stood close without touching each other. Our breaths came and went to the same rhythm. Our hearts were full. Silent and watchful, we waited for them to overflow.

Have you ever seen a water carrier with his leather bag full to bursting with the river's bounty? Sometimes the contents trickle out at the seams, like sweat on the skin of the water bag. So it was with our breaths, with the sound of our hearts. One of us would breathe deeper, or harder, or faster, and then the other's breath would echo and obey the impulse of the first. We stood together, saying nothing, thinking nothing, enveloped by a love so pure and true that we dared not address it.

Time stood suspended, then took itself to a different world. Across the hill, flashes of spring lightning illuminated the sky but there was no sound. The air was charged with power. Lord Varuna was playing with his thunderbolt. In the quiet between us, I heard the rustle of my hair, the slither of his tongue in my ear, the sounds of my welcome as he mounted me.

9

 I do not know when the dreams of night vanished into day, when it came to be dawn, how we returned home. It was oppressive in the house, for she was there. I did not braid my hair again; I would not let her. I left it loose and flowing about my shoulders. I adorned it with buds of hibiscus, and wore the flowers of the sirish in my ears as ornaments. In the warm days I sat in the grove of lemon trees and watched the river. In the nights we made love. It was tender and polite but it was not as it had been in the old temple.

In the evenings I went to the cowsheds to help with the milking. Holding the firm udders, I felt the fine squirt of warm milk on my skin before directing it to the wooden pail. I talked to noble Dasyu, and allowed her to lick my face with her gravelly tongue. I sat in the cowshed thinking of my husband and wondered whether the seed of our love had finally settled within me, if it was at last growing into the life we needed.

One evening, as I was leaving the cowshed to return to

the house, a serpent emerged from the grass and insinuated itself towards Dasyu. It reached for her udder and stood coiled there, greedily drinking her milk. Dasyu was unperturbed, gracious as ever about being robbed. Frozen with fear, I did not scream or call for help. After the serpent had extracted its fill it slithered back into the woods.

It returned the next evening. I was by the door, where the air was heavy with the odour of dung mixed with the fragrance of earth and the sharp tang of the first lemon-blossoms. The serpent came, at the appointed moment, slithering in no further than a single handspan from my feet, and drank directly from Dasyu's teats. I watched intently, trying to decipher what the visitation might mean, but I could understand nothing and was filled with a sense of unease.

When I asked my friend Kundan the meaning of the omen, he replied, 'It means that the snake was thirsty, and in need of nourishment. Furthermore, that the cow was generous and trusting.' He would say no more, and told me not to disturb the fish with my prattle.

I visited the village priest and requested him to interpret the omen. He was more forthcoming. 'See what must be seen, young lady!' he exclaimed. 'Do what must be done!' After some more elliptical introductory remarks, he offered to conduct a prayer on my behalf, a pious invocation in accord with the desires of heaven and earth, to redress the cruel ambitions of a certain young lady. 'Birds are snared in nets, and antelopes in pits,' he said meaningfully, 'but the hearts of kind men are trapped by the wiles of wicked women.'

'There are always remedies against fate,' he explained. 'For every will and destiny there is another conflicting and opposing one. Each of us must do what is best in our place and situation.' He was the same village priest who had propitiated the household fires during the Agnicayana prayers in the fields above the river. I could not believe how much my life had changed in that short time. 'There are means to aid the righteous in their battle with the unrighteous,' he continued, 'and I am here to help you, for you are the birth-sister of the holy monk Guresvara. Bring me a nail from your husband's toe, a hair from the crown of his head, and yes, a piece of cloth torn from your rival's garments, and I shall mend your fate for you.'

I had gone only to enquire about the nature of the omen, but here I was, committed to a path of active retribution I was not sure I believed in. It took me two days to bring him what he had asked for, and some coins from the jar in the hollow of the wall, the gold which my beloved husband in his unfailing generosity had never denied me.

'May you be the mother of a thousand sons!' the priest intoned. 'May your daughters be married to victorious kings!' I had always found him ridiculous, and his posturing prayers only made me despise him the more. He cleared his throat self-consciously before concluding his invocations. 'Take this pathya seedling. On the next moonless night, you must plant it in soil that has first been smeared with vermilion. Come to me on the dawn of the next morning, without eating or drinking anything. Success shall surely attend your endeavours!'

Despite my doubts I did as he instructed. My mother had told me of the magical properties of the pathya, the holy hemp. On the first morning after the new moon I found myself in the temple under the pipala tree where the priest conducted his business. 'Did you implant the sacred pathya?' he asked. He seemed a little sleepy still, and I did not frankly believe that he could move the powers of heaven and earth, invoke the great causal one who grinds the wheels of karma and dharma to take sides with me in my battle with a handmaiden.

There was a havan kund, a circular fire pit, at the side of the temple. The priest set up the ritual flame, not in the traditional way by striking two flint stones, but in the lazier and more convenient manner, using a lit ember from the temple fire and fanning it until it was aflame.

'Now, let me see,' he said abstractedly, 'what was it we were to do? The verses to destroy the rival, I think. Now, how do they go?' He hummed a quatrain to himself. 'No, no, not that one!' He deliberated a little while longer, until his face lit up. 'Let us begin!' he said, and throwing some wood shavings and ghee into the sacrificial fire he began on the Sapatvasana, the invocation to destroy rival wives.

As the sun rises, so my happy sun rises high!
I am victorious, and my lord is submissive to my will!
My sons are slayers of the foe, my daughter is a reigning
queen!
I am victorious over my lord, my song of triumph is now
supreme.

Oblations these have I offered, O gods!
So rid me of each rival wife!
Destroyer of my rival wife, sole spouse, victorious
conqueror;
The other's glory I have seized!
The wealth and beauty of all weaker women—
Be these now mine!

The recitation was full of sound and fury. The tone, pitch or fervour of the rendition could not be faulted. In conclusion, the priest blew vigorously upon a carved conch shell, giving out a long melancholy battle-wail, which echoed across the parallel hills.

But this could not be the right verse for my situation. 'There has been a mistake,' I ventured. 'You see, I have no children. No slayer-of-the-foe sons, no reigning-queen daughter.'

'Aha—of course, of course,' the priest responded. 'Now, let us see . . .' He began again. The sacrificial fire had begun to smoke, and my eyes were watering. More ghee, more wood shavings, and the flames rose to life again.

'Don't worry, sister Shakuntala, this is the correct invocation,' he said consolingly, his high-pitched voice laced uncharacteristically with kindness. Clearly he was moved by my situation, and I was in turn touched by his concern.

From out the earth I dig this plant, a herb of most
effectual power
Wherewith one quells the rival wife and gains the husband
for oneself.

Ever auspicious, with expanded leaves, sent by the gods,
victorious plant,
Blow the rival wife away, and make my husband only
mine!
Her very name I utter not: she takes no pleasure in this
man,
Into the far distance most remote I drive the rival wife
away.
I am the conqueror; and Thou, Thou also are victorious.
As victory attends us both we will subdue my fellow-wife.
I have gained Thee, grasped Thee with a stronger spell
As a cow hastens to her calf, so let Thy spirit speed to me,
hasten like water on its way!

He finished with a flourish and threw a last spoon of ghee on the dying fire. 'Is that better, sister Shakuntala?' he enquired. 'Does that make you happier?'

'It is a child I want,' I said wistfully. 'A child would change everything.'

'You are but a child yourself!' he exclaimed. 'Wait a while until I get some more herbs.' He disappeared into the woods behind the temple, and brought back some pathya leaves, the cure-all for everything from coughs to consumption. 'Just to be careful,' he explained, and began humming to himself all over again.

I saw you pondering in your heart, praying that your
body might be fruitful.
Come, youthful woman, may you spread in your offspring,
you who crave children!

In plants and herbs, in all existent beings
I have deposited the germ of growth.
All progeny on earth have I engendered,
All the sons and warriors who will be hereafter!

He recited it in a hurry this time, without any frills or flourishes. Tying a strand of durbha grass woven into a bracelet upon my left wrist, he anointed my forehead with vermilion and husked rice. Then he took a mangled flower and placed it on my head, and rose hastily to his feet to bless me.

'May the protection of Savitri stay with you!' he concluded, switching from the high Sanskrit of the Vedas to the softer consonants of our spoken dialect. 'I am worried about you, sister Shakuntala,' he said. 'You wander about the woods at night, far from your hearth and home and respected husband. You while away your time with that foolish fisherman and forget the duties of a woman and a wife. The mahasamant Srijan is a mighty man, a wealthy man. Why is it you are not happy?'

What was it I could say? How could I properly respond? 'I want to see the world,' I said awkwardly. Even to my own ears it sounded preposterous. 'I want to travel, as the menfolk do.'

'Look at your feet, Shakuntala,' the priest said solemnly. 'The soles of your feet are decorated with red alta. The toe rings indicate your contentment in marriage. Your anklets weigh down your feet to keep you rooted in your home and family. Men are the masters of women. Your father protects you in childhood, your husband protects you in youth, and your sons protect you in old age; a woman is never fit for independence, that is not the way of the world. You are fortunate to be a rich young woman, without cares or worries. Never forget your good fortune. It is not auspicious.'

When I returned to the house it was already mid-morning. Kamalini was pressing Srijan's feet. She rose hastily as I entered and left the room. Srijan's face lit up when he saw me. 'Dearest wife,' he exclaimed, 'you grow more beautiful every day! I see a special light upon your face, the glow of a woman about to bear fruit.'

The days were light after that, and my senses keener. Parrots chattered and cavorted in the guava trees, the spring songs of the cuckoo celebrated the season. The air was fragrant with breezes from kimsuka groves, and palasha trees heavy with moist red blossoms drooped gracefully in the forest. The news spread through the household that I was with child. I neither confirmed nor denied it.

I remembered the night of love Srijan and I had spent at the abandoned temple. The Matrikas would bless me with a child. I did not need the anxious prayers and fevered exhortations of the village priest. I thought of Dasyu and her calf, and knew with joy and clarity that we would have a daughter whom we would cherish. Great blessings and good fortune would come to us.

The maid Amala, who was responsible for threshing the supplies of corn, came to me excitedly. 'I have a sister who lives down the river,' she said. 'She has told me of a rock that stands in the middle of the Ganga, near the holy temple at Gangadwar. It is a sacred stone, blessed by the gods, which protects virtuous wives and grants them safe childbirth. You must visit this shrine, my lady, and offer your prayers there.'

I had not been to the women's room for three moons now. People around me took this as further, and absolute, proof of the fact that I was pregnant. Yet I felt uncertain about my condition. Unexplained fears and anxiety was keeping me awake at night.

'On the eleventh day of the ascending moon, you must go to this spot to offer flowers and oblations of milk,' Amala continued. 'I will tell the master that it must be done.'

Srijan had a throbbing in his left eye and arm. It was not a good omen, but he insisted that I depart on the appointed day. Amala fed me a madhu-mantha of cooked grains mixed with curd and honey, and marked my forehead with vermilion and sandalwood. As I was about to leave, my right eye began throbbing with nervousness, but Amala assured me that it was only my imagining.

10

 I remember it all as if it were yesterday. On a stone-dry morning in the month of Vaishakh, the palanquin is brought out and four bearers summoned from the fields. They are feeble men, all four, and one of them has a lump the size of a lemon on his brow. Kamalini and I slide into the carved wooden box curtained with cloth and bamboo. Kamalini is too tall to fit comfortably into the palanquin, and her discomfort amuses me.

The landscape passes us by in jumpy snatches. The men on whose shoulders we are travelling downhill begin a song; sweet and melancholy, as hill songs are. I glimpse a lone peacock cross the overgrown path behind us.

Not long into our journey, my bladder is full, and I need desperately to relieve myself. I tell the palanquin-bearers to stop. Dismounting, I disappear into the glade by the side of the path. The river glistens and trembles through the summer haze. On the hill opposite I can see the house where our daughter will grow to womanhood and our sons learn the path of valour and wisdom. I think of the cows in the cowsheds, the pink guavas in the orchard behind the house and the groves of flowering hibiscus in front. As I return to the palanquin, my heart overflows with joy and contentment.

It is past the middle of the day when we reach the bend in the road that Amala described to me, where a steep footpath leads down to the river bed. I tell the men to halt there and await my return. I must walk alone, I do not want Kamalini with me while I pray for my child, so I tell her to stay back as well. I find that I can instruct Kamalini quite easily when I am away from home and from Srijan. Needless to say, I have never been so far away from home—not, at least, in the direction of the plains.

The shore is pebbled here, not sandy; and its smooth white stones burn hot on my bare soles. But the river is cool and welcoming. She laps and pulls at me, the undercurrents like playful snakes slithering around my feet, insinuating their way up my legs. I discard my cumbersome silver anklets and leave them on the shore. Suddenly, I am free. I will wear them again only when it is time to return home.

A makeshift crossing of wood and boulders leads to the temple, which juts out of a crash of waves. Unsteadily balancing the pitcher of milk and a basket of flowers in my hands, I make my way there. The sun is at its zenith; it shines in my eyes, blinding me with its splendour. An expanse of flat land stretches out on either side of me, seemingly forever. Everything looks different. The low bushes and squat trees do not reach out for the skies as they do in our forests. The

Ganga, too, is transformed. No longer a moody mountain stream, she is mature, powerful, sure of herself. Deep in the horizon, where the river meets the sky, a white sail flutters in the breeze.

I make my way up the slippery steps. A flat, unpolished rock sustains a Shiva-lingam of dark river stone, the three auspicious stripes on it occurring in natural formation: Narbadeshwar, it is called, though it could not have been rolled oval by the Narbada River. Standing before it, I am distracted by the ordinariness of it and for a brief moment wonder why I am here. Then I remember and offer the flowers, scarlet hibiscus and yellow champaka blossoms, and milk from noble Dasyu. Pouring the milk over the lingam as ceremoniously as I can, I try to think holy, exalted thoughts. But all the odds and ends of prayer and magical verse I know have evaporated, disappeared from memory. I remember nothing. The only image that rises in my mind is one of the anthill on the way to the abandoned temple, the line of ants marching in precise formation on the grass.

I can hear the Ganga lapping at the rocks, licking and kissing the black stones. The water glints in the sun, the waves chase each other. I have not known so much silence; there is nothing over the sound of water, not even a birdcall. Nor have I ever had so much of the world to myself, for here I am alone, with only the river and the rocks below and the sky above me. I search for the white sail of the riverboat I glimpsed earlier, but it has vanished.

I return to the shore, and before I leave the water, turn

to look out across the river, into the horizon that could be the end of the world or some great city, Kashi or Pataliputra. I hear a soft splash behind me, and the sound of laughter. I turn around. A man is standing by the river. My eyes are already dazzled by the play of sunlight on the water, and when I see him my head spins. Perhaps it is the shock of finding him there, the only person other than me between river and sky. The intimacy of the moment is almost illicit. He is short, with muscular thighs and stocky calves and the curliest hair I have ever seen, and he is dressed differently from all the men I know: sandals with upturned toes are strapped to his ankles, and a short tunic is tied at his waist with an elaborate leather belt. He looks utterly carefree, reckless and happy; his square, firm face holds a baffling merriment, and I know, instinctively, that he has travelled for long and through many worlds to be here. He smiles at me. I am enchanted by his smile.

I walk towards him. A sturdy bay horse with a splash of white on its forehead, like a star, is tethered to the tree behind. The man says nothing, he does not greet me or ask who I am. Holding on to the reins of the horse with one hand, he encircles me with his free arm and kisses me. Our tongues meet and circle like waves on the river. It is the most natural and inevitable thing in the world. My mind feels empty as the pitcher in my hand, and vast as the sky above. I know that somewhere just up the hill, Kamalini is waiting for me with the palanquin-bearers. It is an absurd and unnecessary detail from another life.

He asks what sounds like a question. At first I cannot recognize the language he speaks. Sensing my confusion, he switches to Prakrit, pronouncing the words of the dialect slowly, carefully, with an unfamiliar accent. They remain suspended; mere sounds, birds in flight. I can barely decipher what they might mean. The horse stands behind me, its hot breath whispering in my ears. The stranger's eyes are grey— or are they blue? Are they a cloudy sky that has not decided which way the weather will go? Like thunderclouds, they are rimmed with a dark line of kohl, the eye-salve accentuating their startling colour. We lay ourselves on the river shore. The sun shines bright in the sky. We do not go through the set motions of desire and arousal, there are no love bites or coy looks or sly smiles. We scramble into each other as rabbits into their burrows. We are instinct itself. He empties himself into me, pours the ritual oblation upon my yoni. I have never felt so alone, so absolutely only-myself, unmoored from everyone and everything familiar. My life has changed; I feel that I cannot go back to where I have come from.

Every limb in my body is alive, and yet I am rested and satiated. Nothing has prepared me for this ecstasy. It defies my life and destiny, disengaging it from the wheel of duty and dharma and what should be, throwing it directly into my own hands.

'My name is Nearchus and I am from the land of the Yavanas,' he tells me in Prakrit. I struggle to understand his words. 'Nearchus,' I repeat the name after him. I know nothing about Yavanas except that they are mlechhas, unclean foreigners whose presence can pollute the penance and prayers of high-born castes. 'Come with me, river-goddess,' he continues. 'I want to flow in your waters forever.' It sounds hyperbolic and insincere, even comical, but in the timelessness of that moment I want to believe him—and perhaps he does too. He is whispering something in my ear again, but in a strange tongue. His Yavana breath is sweet, smelling of pine needles and things green. As his lips touch my earlobe, my stomach contracts over with desire. His mouth moves to mine, the kiss searching so deep that when at last I disentangle myself, something of me is left behind in him forever.

He is young, and the sun has only ripened his skin, not aged it yet. His hair, the soft stubble on his chin, is brown-gold, like fox hair. I stroke his face tenderly, even while the memory of a woman named Shakuntala, the life that she lived, nudges at me. Two voices rise within. One guiding me to return home, away from this violation, this absolute mockery of the matrimonial promises of love. The other, buzzing about my ears like a bhramari, a lascivious bee, urges me to flee, run away as far and as fast as I can, before Kamalini and the palanquin-bearers, intruders from another life, come in search of me.

I look at the river, as if to find an answer in her waves, and my eyes fall upon the silver anklets I have left by the shore. Disentangling myself from the Yavana's embrace I bend down to retrieve them. Their familiar weight settles upon my feet, and I am Shakuntala again. The anklets beat out their resolute music as I tread the path home.

'Come back, river-goddess!' the Yavana cries lustily. I do not look back. 'I know you will come,' he says. 'Tomorrow, yes, you will come to me. I shall be waiting for you here, by the river.' A metallic echo returns his words to me, like the undertow of the waves.

The palanquin-bearers are asleep. They lie in different poses of abandon, mouths agape, the sounds of their snoring drowning the distant roar of the river. I stare at them, irresolute.

A fly falls into the blameless mouth of Manomath, the oldest of the bearers. He wakes up with a start, gasping and choking. I make my way to the palanquin. Kamalini is seated inside, and the bamboo interior is choked with the cloying scents of musk and roses. Lazily, her eyes acknowledge my presence. She moves slightly to one side to accommodate me. There is an infuriating graciousness in the gesture. I can still feel the Yavana's kisses upon my lips.

The slow dusk crept in as we made our way home, held up in the shaking cage. By the time we returned, it was dark. Srijan appeared preoccupied. He greeted me with a hasty formality, his eyes focussed above mine, behind, where she stood. We retired to lie together in our chamber, confronting not each other but the shadows of our loves. Srijan's lips bruised the spots fevered by the Yavana's touch. Did he seek me as he probed and thrust, or my handmaiden Kamalini?

I do not know. I rode my desires, uncaring of his comfort. At the height of our passion he held himself back.

'You are with child, Shakuntala,' he said. 'It is not the time for love-making.'

He nestled me in his arms. I felt stifled, crowded by the unfailing regularity of his breathing, every inhalation always twice the length of the exhalation. Quietly, so as not to wake him, I left our bed. The oil lamp that wavered by the wall had long since been extinguished. I walked around the room, every corner of which I knew so well, and measured my way to the window. Outside, I could hear the sounds of night, the owls rustling in the mulberry tree, the river thrashing its banks. The tinkling of my anklets woke up my husband. Sleepily, he called for me.

I would not go back to him. The night beckoned, and the river, and my old thirst for I knew not what. Srijan was asleep again, unheeding of my absence. I stayed awake until the dawn, when I retreated briefly to his side. 'I had a dream this morning,' I lied to my husband when he awoke. 'I must go once more to the temple at Gangadwar and offer my prayers.'

Dhania arrived with a present for me. It was a caged mina bird, with dark wings and inscrutable eyes. The cage was crafted with bamboo and bent cane. 'You can spend your time at home teaching him to speak,' Dhania said. 'You should not be roaming around the hills alone in your condition.'

From the window I could see the sky. It was grey, approaching blue, like the Yavana's eyes. 'I must go again to Gangadwar,' I told my husband.

'Can you not go tomorrow?' he asked.

'Tomorrow will be too late,' I replied.

Amala was summoned to call the palanquin-bearers from the village. 'There is still time,' I told myself. I looked around, at the familiarity that was no longer comforting, my gaze as worn as the oak beam that marked the threshold of the house. What was here to hold me back? Not Srijan's love, as lying as a mina's chatter.

'You are with child,' a voice within me whispered. 'There is still time.'

The mina let out an untutored squawk. Dhania placed a quartered guava in its cage. 'Love in a cage, is love in a rage . . .' she was humming. I had never heard the song before. What did she know? And why did it matter so little to me that she did? The mina screeched. My head was spinning from all the noise.

'Send for Kamalini to comb my hair,' I said to Dhania. I needed to look my best, of that I was certain. I anointed my breasts with sandal oil, and folded a silk antariya to take along with me. 'My clothes may get wet, the river is unpredictable,' I explained weakly, although Dhania had not asked.

Kamalini entered to comb and braid my hair. Her fingers were hostile. She pulled and twisted until I cried out in pain. 'Can you not be gentle?' I said reprovingly.

'I am not well,' Kamalini replied sulkily. 'Can you not take Amala or Kudari to Gangadwar with you?'

At this provocative response I flew into a rage. 'So you can stay here alone with your master?' I screamed. I was shaking, like the string of a bow after the arrow has fled.

'I am not the one who seeks his attention,' she said

insolently. 'I shall come if you instruct me to.'

As we left I looked back at the house. Amala and Dhania were standing outside, gossiping. They had forgotten to keep my silk antariya in the palanquin.

And Srijan, where was he? I should have waited to see him, to leave with him watching me go. But I was in a hurry to get away now.

The palanquin-bearers were silent till I put my head out and asked them to sing. They obliged, with a song about a bride leaving her mother's home. We were by the riverside before the sun was too high. 'As you are not well, it is best that you rest here,' I said sarcastically to Kamalini. She yawned, and stretched sensuously.

I walked down the path. As I reached the river, I could hear his laughter. Taking off my silver anklets, I flung them into the water and ran towards him. The Yavana led me to his horse. He mounted it with a quick graceful motion and pulled me up behind him. My arms settled around the serrated leather belt on his waist and I fell into rhythm with the movement of the animal. On that pebbled shore I left Shakuntala and all her memories.

11

 Behind us are the hills, a purple smudge growing more distant with every forward movement of the horse. My hair flies about my face and my eyes sting with tears, provoked by the hot breeze and some profound emotion that resembles sorrow. Unfastening the leather flask hanging from the Yavana's shoulder, I drink deeply of it. The flask is filled not with water, but with a sweet, rich wine. My senses, strained already to their very optimum, are both lulled and stimulated by its heady joys. I tighten my grip around the Yavana's waist and press against his back. He laughs and shouts out—a command or an endearment, I cannot be sure. The horse begins to race faster into the plains.

It was already mid-afternoon when we fled from the riverbank. Following the meandering course of the Ganga, we reached a larger, wider path, in turn forking into two further lanes. Nearchus got off his horse. I tumbled down after him and shook the dust from my clothes. He muttered what seemed to be a prayer, then picked up a pebble and flung it behind him. 'The goddess of the underworld blesses the paths of travellers wherever three roads meet,' he explained. 'Hecate guides them through the past, the present, and the future.'

But I had no concept of past and future any more. Each moment, lighter than air, existed only in itself, unhinged from everything before and after. I looked at him as he spoke, my senses sharpened by the wine from his flask. An embroidered cape was furled around his short tunic. A dagger and a bunch of keys hung from his leather belt. A gold chain shone around the burnished column of his neck, a signet ring glittered on his little finger. It seemed beyond comprehension, and yet natural, that I should be with him, that I should want to taste the sweat on his skin.

He slipped the ring off his finger. 'Take it,' he said. 'It belongs to you as I do.' I wore the ring, but it was too loose for me, and I returned it to him.

'This ring belonged to my father,' he said, climbing on to his horse and holding a hand out for me. 'He was banished to an oasis in the Libyan desert. He gave it to me before he left. I never saw him alive again.'

I took his hand and clambered on after him. The horse raced on, as if we had never stopped.

'What is an oasis?' I asked. 'And the Libyan desert?'

'It is a place in the sands of Afrid,' the Yavana explained. 'After my father was sent away when I was eleven, I became groom to a great nobleman. I tamed a spirited horse for him, and became his favourite servant, travelling with him to Afrid and Egypt. Then we came to Serindia to trade, through the lands of Magna Grecia and Persia, and I worked as his agent, procuring and forwarding all kinds of things at his behest. But my master died, and I stayed on, buying and selling horses. Me and my steed, Arion, whose saddle you grace, have made this land our own.'

He spoke haltingly, and the wind on our faces and the speed at which the horse tore down the road threw his words into the receding landscape. I asked him no more questions, for I had no pictures in my mind for the places and things he talked of. Instead I observed my surroundings. The roads we travelled were raised above the surface of the adjacent land. By the sides of these were ditches lined with sand, and then a patchwork of carefully tended fields. The fields were guarded by scarecrows fashioned from buffalo skeletons set up on poles. We sped past carts and wagons piled high with fruits, both green and ripe. Shady trees lined the road, protecting us from the worst excesses of the afternoon sun.

By nightfall we reached a halting-house on the banks of the Ganga. A gilded horse-drawn carriage stood grandly by the entrance. Beside it, a line of tired oxen were tethered to wooden posts. The flaming torches at the doorway, the marble urns outside the courtyard all appeared very splendid. I looked around anxiously to sight an elephant, but there was none. Determined not to betray my ignorance, I followed Nearchus in as though we had been travelling together all our lives.

The innkeeper seemed to know him well, and appeared not at all surprised to see me. We were escorted to a resting-chamber, equipped with a mattress and night lamp. The room smelt of human and animal odours, and the cloying fumes of incense. I was gagging from the stench, and the heat was making me dizzy. My body was soaked in sweat. The madness which had possessed me had not yet waned. My senses were on fire, and I was impatient to lie with the Yavana and begin our love-play again. He was as eager as I was, and we fell on the mattress and each other with a fervour that did not abate all night. Only when we were utterly drained, when the Ushas were already groping in the sky and the dawn fumbling towards its appointment with daylight, did he ask me what my name was.

'Yaduri,' I replied without hesitation. It was the name of an old woman who had sometimes assisted my mother in her healing work. Nearchus found my reply hilarious. He broke into uncontrollable laughter, rolling about the tiny room in mirth. 'Yaduri,' he roared, 'what an appropriate name!' Only much later did I realize that, in the swearing and profane language of men, the word also signified a yoni, a woman's private part. Having asked me my name, which caused him such amusement, he did not question me any further on my situation or my past. I too remained silent, keeping the story of Shakuntala and her life from his knowledge, for he had no use for it.

The innkeeper woke us before dawn. 'There are rumours of bandits,' he said to Nearchus. 'It is best for you to travel with a convoy. A caravan leaves here soon, and for a small fee you can ride with them.'

Sleepily we left the room, and watched the caravan prepare for the journey. A thick chorus of birds, such as I had never heard in the mountains, erupted from the squat, stunted trees. The sartha, the leader of the group, greeted us, looked at me with some interest, and then returned his attention to the wagons and draught animals. The oxen and the sleek buffaloes were fed and given water. The wheels of the carts were carefully oiled, enormous jars of water and chests of provisions listed and loaded. As the first hint of light appeared in the sky, the grinding of wooden wheels and the slow rhythmic tread of the bullock carts brought the procession to life. We spent the day travelling. The caravan raised a thick dust that made my eyes burn. At nightfall, we stopped at a clearing in the forest. The carts were drawn up in a circle, with the animals penned to the centre. Fires were lit around the camp. The men took turns to mount guard, in prahars, watches of six hours each.

I was the only woman in the group. The other travellers maintained a courteous distance. They would not eat with us, for the caste rules of the varna dharma forbade them from dining with mlechhas and impure foreigners. 'I cannot understand the ways of your people,' Nearchus complained. 'Even in battle, they continue to cook separately, each soldier tending to his own fire pot for fear of caste pollution. Who can win a war like that? And yet, I have encountered a Yavana from my land who was promoted to a Brahmin by your priests. It is a strange land!'

Content to be left alone, we slept in the open and watched the stars. The sky-river, the Mandakini, shone like an arc of incandescent light. I searched for the Arundhati star, the vision of constancy to which a man, long ago, had tried to guide his young wife. A stab of hurt accompanied the memory. I was Yaduri now, I had abandoned both Srijan and Shakuntala. The heavens were so bright and yet so far away. They seemed to forgive everything we mortals did. There was great consolation in their distance.

I found the familiar constellation of the thrice-knotted arrow in the crowd of stars and pointed it out to Nearchus. 'It cannot be!' he exclaimed. 'That's the girdle of Orion, not an arrow. And the red star that gleams like a mad dog's eye in the centre is Sirius, the Dog Star. When the Dog Star rises, the lands around the river Aigyptos are consumed by floods.' It still looked like an arrow to me, not like a dog's eye, and I reflected upon how different people could see and understand the same things so differently.

We set off again at dawn. The sun rose over the fields and glittered on the canals that flowed beside the road. Neatly marked pillars demarcated the distance. The convoy halted at a toll-point where the antapala, the official in charge of roads, was stationed to collect taxes from the caravans and processions travelling on royal highways.

'It seems the kings of Kanauj and Maha Koshala are busy raising revenues so that they can begin a war again!' Nearchus exclaimed. 'As for me, I would rather pay robbers than kings.' We left the caravan and followed a narrow side-path to avoid the toll-point. My companion evidently knew the road well, for after fording a shallow river and cantering through a rutted by-lane we were on the main highway again.

We spent the next day travelling. The road sped behind us like a fleeing thief. The landscape was flat and monotonous. The red mead in the Yavana's flask aggravated rather than slaked my thirst. It was intolerably hot, and we stopped to rest by the banks of the Ganga. An evening breeze rose to ripple across the water. I felt an intense sense of homecoming. Contentedly, I washed and cleansed myself by the shore of this river that had nurtured me from birth. Arion nibbled on the young foliage while we retreated to a shaded bower of vines and flowers. As I lay with the Yavana among the fragrant beds of madhavi and madhumalti, I thought of my namesake Shakuntala, sleepily reclining by the creeper-wreathed banks of the Malini River, bracelets of lotus buds circling her wrists, tender sirish flowers hanging from her ears. Thinking of her, I plucked a blossom of scarlet hibiscus and placed it behind my ear, even though I knew it would wilt with the evening. Perhaps I looked beautiful.

Nearchus was insatiable in his desires. He did not tire or yield, though his hunger was blind, far greater than his ability to satisfy it. My thighs were sore from the repeated force of his attacks, my buttocks hurt from the vigorous movements of the horse, my calves were bruised from the pressure of the stirrups. There was pleasure and pain in this love-making.

I awoke briefly as the dawn was breaking in the eastern quarter. My lover was asleep beside me, his eyeballs shifting agitatedly in their sockets. He was murmuring in his dreams, uttering strange sentences in a language I did not understand. For a moment his sleeping face broke into a sob. I put my hand on his brow, and his features became calm with my touch.

The next day, and the next, and the next. Forests, fields, and water chased each other with untiring regularity. We passed boats and rafts on the Ganga, loaded with passengers and merchandise. On the highways, we met horse carts and ox wagons, caravans and convoys. I saw a procession of camels, tall, awkward creatures wearing expressions of intolerable pride. Nearchus mimicked their countenance, looking so like a camel himself that I laughed until my stomach hurt. And then, from the corner of my eye, I glimpsed an enormous beast. It was even larger than I had expected. The lugubrious, swaying gait left me enchanted. 'An elephant!' I shouted, almost falling off Arion in my excitement.

'The elephants in your country are magnificent!' Nearchus declared. 'As for the mahouts of these imperial beasts, they are an inspiration to the world. The land of the Ganga surpasses all others in the glory of its elephants and trainers. I have ridden on elephants in the sands of Libya, where my father died, and by the river Aigyptos, and they are as different from the ones here as a mouse is from a rat!'

'Tell me more,' I said breathlessly.

'Well, the male covers the female in a most peculiar way,' he continued mock-seriously, his eyes alight with suppressed laughter. 'The she-elephant must pay for these joys by carrying her babies, one at a time, for fourteen to eighteen months. Moreover, these unfortunate animals live for a hundred years, and sometimes even two hundred, unlike me who will have bid this world farewell by the time I reach thirty!'

The mrighastin's eyes met mine. They were quiet, wise. I could not hold their knowing gaze; they reminded me of someone. I shut my eyes and clutched on to the Yavana, as the tinkle of the elephant-bell grew gentler and more distant.

Days and nights of travel, the river a constant by our side. The exhilaration of the adventure was beginning to wear off. Summer had arrived, early and abruptly, and I was in the plains for the first time in my life. Great fires raged in the sky through the day; hot dust rose around us as we rode, and settled on our clothes and in our hair. I was exhausted, it took all my resolve simply to remain in the saddle, to hold on to Nearchus and continue the interminable journey. At the time of godhuli, the cow-dust hour when the cattle returned home, the tinkle of their bells, the certainty of their direction reminded me of home. I began to depend on the sweet-tasting mead to keep the sadness at bay.

We were riding along the riverbank. The rutted road was verged with dry, brown grass. The whisper of a flute broke through the gloaming. I looked around in search of the unknown flautist, but could see no one. Tall river reeds swayed in the evening breeze. The last of the summer crops stood to our right. Some were already harvested, the remaining stalks wilting in the molten heat. As we travelled, the sound of the flute persisted and followed us. Abruptly, Nearchus reined the horse in. I tried to hold on to him, but he was already dismounting, swearing angrily. Somehow I got my stiff limbs to obey me, and struggled down to the ground. A man lay on the path before us, as though asleep, or drunk, or dead. His mouth was curled into a grimace, which could well have been a bitter smile. One eye was closed, as though he were winking at the heavens. Even as I protested, Nearchus turned him over with a swift movement of his foot. His skull was smashed from the back, where the blood had congealed into a mass of pulpy vermilion.

That landscape has followed me in nightmares. A drenched amber sky, swaying river reeds, a melancholy flute-song streaming out from an unknown source. Nearchus bent down and gently put the corpse straight. Then something came over him, a great, futile gust of anger. He clenched his fists tight and kicked the corpse off the road into the field below. Mounting the horse, he pulled me up behind him.

The music continued to haunt us. It was getting to be dark, but the memory of the sun lingered on the horizon, the earth still burned from the rage of the day. We stopped again. Another motionless figure lay barring our path. Nearchus dismounted and I tumbled down after him. The corpse was charred black, a heap of dead, foul-smelling flesh so obscene and startling that the mead I had drunk rose inside me in a sour wave. I was vomiting by the side of the road, and as for the Yavana, he was angrier than ever, cursing and shouting in his foreign tongue. He did not kick the body this time. We mounted the horse and rode carefully over it. The echo of the flute followed us. Our eyes had adjusted to the darkness, when I saw a glow of light. Billowing flames lit up a crowd of crazed faces. A man was on fire, his torched frame writhing in agony. Howls and gulps of anger rose from the mob around him; they were threatening him still. I could smell the wood, the acrid smoke, the stench of roasting flesh and burnt hair. The mob did not seem to notice our arrival. They were self-absorbed, intent on themselves, on the man they were killing. He staggered about in a jerky dance, imploring arms outstretched, before he fell on the ground.

Abruptly, the crowd composed itself. They held their torches aloft, and lined up by the side of the road to let us pass. Arion was neighing nervously. Nearchus was reining him in. I could sense that he too was afraid. I was soaked in sweat, and the taste of vomit was lodged in my throat. We rode on for a while before Nearchus and Arion cut through the tall, tangled thickets of river-grass, and we were by the Ganga. The moon had not risen, but I could hear the dark water. Also the sound of the flute; it had persisted and followed us here. I saw a boat with a light by its prow, and then, finally, faintly, the flautist, coaxing his reed instrument into the saddest sounds.

'If they follow us, jump into the river,' Nearchus whispered. The unknown musician had seen us. He navigated his boat into the shallows and scrambled out. If he was surprised to see Yavana, horse and woman in the night, by the sacred water, he did not betray his surprise.

'Your neighbours on the shore seem very fond of murder,' Nearchus said curtly. His hand was by his belt, levering the knife he kept there.

'It's the same story every year,' the reed-thin boatman replied. 'The summer arrives, scorching the earth. The grass and foliage die. Then the cattle starve. The Bomariya tribes skin them, and use the skin for their trade. Sometimes, they kill the starving cattle, without waiting for them to die. It is summer, it is unbearably hot, the Yadavas and cow-herders are as inflamed as the low-caste Bomariyas. They kill them first and invent the reasons and excuses later. More widows, more carcasses. I like to stay on the water, playing my flute. Their shore is not my place.'

The moon was up now, just above the river, heavy, yellowed, already weary. Clumps of moon-lotus unfolded by the banks. We shared our food between us. We ate bread from the Yavana's satchel, and some boiled sorghum which the boatman was carrying. The horse was hungry too. Nearchus fed it with oats and we waited for the night to pass. The boatman offered to let us sleep aboard his craft, but I could see that Nearchus was afraid that we might be murdered, or our horse stolen. I shared his caution and joined him in declining the offer.

A slow breeze was playing on the river, stroking the reeds and bushes by the shore. I was afraid to lie down, for there might be snakes, or scorpions, or river crabs. Or memories. We sat the night out, leaning on each other, my head on Nearchus's shoulder, then his head on my lap, Arion's tether held tight in his clenched fist. I remember the flute playing through the night. It was desolate and sweet, a melody for lost worlds.

12

Yet the world is born anew every morning.
I took to my changed circumstances with ease. I did not think of the house in the mountains. The young woman called Yaduri had no history. She lived in the ceaseless present. Only the river travelled with her, its murmur in her life-blood.

'We will arrive in Kashi soon,' Nearchus said to me. In our travels we had passed villages and settlements and small towns. I hungered to see the greatest city of them all, proud, immortal Kashi. My brother Guresvara had described it often, the temples to Lord Shiva, the burning ghats, the great river of remembrance and forgiveness. Of course, the Kashi he sought was different from the city of towering palaces and golden chariots that I dreamt of.

There were many other cities besides Kashi. There was Pataliputra, with its wooden fortifications, further down the Ganga, and Ujjaini, that gracious and fashionable settlement on the banks of the Narmada. I had heard too of Mathura,

Magadha and Mithila. I asked Nearchus how many cities he
had been to. 'Too many,' he replied laughingly. 'Cities, my
lady, are like beautiful women. After a while they all begin to
appear the same. We shall go to Kashi and dress you in grand
robes. Fine women need fine garments to please them.' He
smiled and his white teeth gleamed in the sun. He took
another deep draught of wine, and gave the flask to me to
share.

I drank from it, eager for the warmth that travelled from
my throat to my body, for the abandonment the wine
provoked. As the sky turned dark, and the stars began to
reveal themselves above us, we got down to kissing lustily.
The Yavana's way of love-making was different from what I
had known in the other life. It was rough and hungry and
even unskilled, yet it aroused me in ways quite contrary to
those I had experienced before. I discovered that I enjoyed
being hurt, and that pain validated my pleasure in matters of
the flesh. The Yavana's uncaring demands for his satisfaction
unleashed my darkest desires. Duty and decorum had fled
me. We fornicated beyond the predictability of animals,
which is after all within the rhythm and understanding of
nature. And still I hungered for more. He took me by the
orifice that lies behind. He held me roughly and slapped me
on the face, his own face twisted in confusion, and told me
that he hated women, they were all sluts and slatterns to the
core, they were not for love. I did not protest, for I had
surrendered to this new fate. His coarse words only excited
me the more. They confirmed my discovery that I was a fallen

woman, and something in me exulted and rejoiced in being so.

Yaduri revelled in the powers of her body. She rode her pleasures with determination, denying the pain that rotted in the core of her self. Pleasure is an inexplicable emotion. Its boundaries recede like the mirage that follows the road by the Ganga on a hot summer day. It is a pursuit; in its moment of consummation its victim is already seeking the next desperate experience. There is a dark shade that stalks us in all our lives, seeking our debasement. It is said that the food we consume in our last life will consume us in the next: perhaps the seeds of Shakuntala's karma carried in them the sad fruit of Yaduri's disobedience.

Yaduri was sweat, salt and desire. Her pleasure spot was greedy and hungry for joy, it could not be satiated. In those moments of forgetting herself, of being swallowed up by her senses, Yaduri forgot who she had once been and perhaps still was.

One night, when he was weak with wine and drunk with something approaching love, Nearchus told me of his homeland, of vineyards that purpled in the summer, and of light as precious as gold. He was gentle with me that night, and we glided in and out of each other as in a dream. He talked of his childhood, the boy he had been, and of Constantinopolis, the city of his birth. 'It is a rough city, excelling at trade and war,' he said, 'ruled in equal part by the emperor and the mob. They seek trade, and victory, wherever they venture. We have a weapon, called Greek fire, of which only the emperors know the secret. Flame-throwers hurl this fire at enemy ships and troops, making our nation invincible. The Arabs have learnt this to their sorrow.'

Hanging on to every word, I asked him about the Yavanas, and how they came to be so far from the lands that were their home. 'Our people have a love of travel,' he replied. 'In the olden days we were blessed by the god of wayfarers, Hermes of the winged foot. He was responsible for the making of treaties, and for trade, and maintaining the right of way for travellers on any road in the world.

'Gods travel too, as we mortals do. At least the old gods did, and they are the gods I still believe in,' he continued. 'When Alexander came to Indika, a thousand years ago, Lord Uranus, god of the sky, travelled with him. He is the one your people know as Varuna. And then there is Heracles, who settled in the mountains of the north and made them his home.'

My home too lay in the mountains. I thought of the hill-foots of the north, my childhood there, all that I had left behind. I banished the thought, and tried instead to picture the vineyards, and the golden light that shone over them.

That night, again, Nearchus muttered and mumbled in his dreams, and wept as though he was suffering a nightmare. There was a name he murmured, in tones of love and anguish. The name was Hippolytus. I listened mutely, and wondered if she had been his wife, his mother or his mistress. I soothed him, stroking his curly golden-brown hair, but he would not be lulled. I even read out the dream charm for

nightmares, the invocation to the Gandharva Vaivasvat, but
my lover seemed caught in some painful event from his past
from which I could not rescue him.

With sunrise, his nightmares departed. He was humming
through his morning rituals. The Yavana had a peculiar habit:
he used a sharp blade to keep his face shorn of masculine
growth. My brother Guresvara shaved both his scalp and his
face, but my husband had always sported a handsome beard.
Nearchus's face had little hair, yet he did not look at all
womanly. I loved the feel of the bristles thrusting through his
skin. As he scraped the blade delicately down his jaw, both
puzzled and pleased by my interest, for I was seated before
him and watching intently, he told me of his further adventures.

He had travelled all through the world. His stories were
improbable but compelling. He told me of places with strange
names, which my brother Guresvara had never seen, nor my
husband in his many travels. He talked of Kabul and Kandahar,
and the mountains of the Hindu Kush where he had seen a
tribe of women bandits who were all blind. The Indus was the
largest of all the rivers in the world after the Aigyptos, he told
me, and the most fearsome. And then there were the Hydaspes,
the Choaspes, the Hyphasis. Of all the rivers that my lover
had seen, he most admired the Danube, a blue river which
flowed to the west of the land of the Yavanas.

'Tell me more about your land,' I pleaded.

'Well, the ladies of Serindia are much admired there,' he
said. 'They are sold by merchants as slaves and dancing girls.
The more distant their origin, the higher their price. The

rapacious Arabs control the slave trade. They sell poor Ionian maidens to the royal harems in your country, where they are employed as handmaidens or military guards.'

I was greedy for these stories, and tried to memorize the strange names he spoke and hold on to them as imagined pictures in my head. Nearchus told me of the ocean, where the rivers go when they leave the land. I could not picture it—water and more water as far as the eye can see! There were waves that roared like thunder, and rose as high as mountains. Greek, Roman and Arab ships sailed on the sea, large wooden houses that did not sink, that could carry horses and even elephants in their holds. The world was a wild and wondrous place, and I was glad to be free and alone and travelling its surface with this Yavana who had seen and known so much.

Nearchus traded in horses, which he procured from the lands of Persia and Araby, or from Khotan, across the snow-mountains. The horse dealers undertook long and dangerous journeys, driving sometimes even five hundred animals to be sold to the royal courts. He told me of wild horses, twice the size of normal horses, that were sought for their tails, fine as a woman's hair. Elegant ladies in the great cities made coiffures and braids of them, intertwining them with their own natural hair. Horsehair on women! I could no longer believe his absurd stories, and begged him not to fool me simply because I knew so little.

'No, my lady, what is true is almost inevitably strange,' he replied. 'Is it not strange, for instance, that you and I, who scarcely know each other, are travelling together across the plains of the Doab?'

I was hungry for knowledge, as a bear for honey. The Yavana did not scorn my curiosity, he did not think it inappropriate of me to ask so many questions. I could have listened forever, even if he were lying. He wove tales of distant lands and people, of Moslems, and Jews, and Manicheans, and Paulicians, of ships and caravans that carried merchandise from Indika across the world. Ivory, the most precious of these items of trade, was crafted into sword hilts and scabbards, hairpins, brooches and birdcages. People in different lands traded in buffalo horn, rhinoceros horn, tortoise shell, mother of pearl, and priceless gems like agate, onyx, ruby, sapphire and emerald. Silk thread from China was woven in India, and cottons from the western ports were sent across the seas to Egypt, to be sold again by the merchants there.

I listened spellbound as he talked knowledgeably of ginger and cinnamon-bark, of camphor leaves and cardamom, cloves and sesame. 'There is much profit to be had in perfumes and incense,' he informed me. 'Sandalwood, myrrh, balsam and cinnabar are more precious than gold. Musk from Tibet is transported by caravans in tightly sealed vases. For the bandits that lie in wait along the travel routes, it is worth more than a king's ransom. There is no end to the things you can buy and sell from Indika. The holds of merchant ships are crammed with peacocks, talking parrots, tame monkeys and even elephants!'

Nearchus was amused by my hunger for the smallest scrap of knowledge or information. 'You are a peculiar woman,' he said. 'You find more pleasure in my tongue than in my kisses! Do you really want to know more about trade and commerce?'

'Although I am neither a merchant nor a tax collector, I want to know everything I possibly can,' I replied. I was not attempting to be humorous, but Nearchus broke into uproarious laughter, crinkling up his eyes and throwing back his head until those long curls touched his shoulders.

'You are probably not a female at all,' he teased. 'You are not vain, you do not complain while travelling, and you take interest in the most unusual things!' I was unsure whether to be hurt or flattered by his description. But I was intoxicated by this utter and absolute freedom, the constant movement, and I was ready to go on and on, until the end of the world if necessary.

13

 I can never forget that first sight of Kashi. We arrived late at night. On the opposite bank, funeral fires blazed on the stepped ghats, the flames inverting on the broken mirror of the waves. Death lived here, I had heard, forever mocking life and its passage. I stared at the shadowed city, above which hung a grave, fiery moon, and shivered with a fierce sense of premonition.

Kashi, the city of Shiva. The faithful arrived here in the hope of departure, for to die in Kashi was to escape the remorseless cycle of birth and rebirth. Shiva, bending over the dead and the dying, whispered his mantra of deliverance into the ears of corpses. The Taraka mantra liberated them, ferried them across the river of oblivion to the far shores of moksha.

I told Nearchus to rein in the impatience of Arion. We dismounted to look at the city of light in all her glory. Here, Shiva, worshipped as Vishwanath, lord of the worlds, ruled as an ash-smeared beggar living in cremation grounds. 'All of creation resides in Kashi,' Guresvara had said, 'although our minds or our hands can no more grasp it than they can clutch a stream of living water.'

We could have stopped at a hostelry at dusk and arrived the next morning, but Nearchus was tired of travelling and eager to reach his destination. I was still wearing the flaxen wrap and antariya in which I had left home. Aware of how grimy and unkempt I appeared, I had attempted to wash my clothes and untangle my hair. My lover stood with his back to me, making water noisily in a ditch, while I held Arion. I had become familiar with his smell, the manner in which he shook his mane, his way of stamping his hooves. Together, we examined the burning pyres, until Nearchus returned and leapt on to the horse.

Here I was, in the holiest of cities, accompanied by a mlechha, an unclean Yavana. 'Kashi is the premier city in all Indika,' Nearchus told me matter-of-factly. 'It extends over twelve leagues, while mighty settlements like Mithila or Pataliputra can boast of only seven. The main city, of course, lies across the river, but we foreigners are quartered on this side of the shore, both for our comfort and to maintain the so-called purity of your Brahmins and high priests.' He smelt of the sweet wine that he carried in his flask, and the exhalations of wine and horse and sweat are forever associated in my mind with the first incredible sight of Kashi.

We rode further, till we were at a discreet white building with a long pool of water spread before it. The reflection of a lamp, so bright that for a moment I mistook it for the moon, paused in the still water that was crowded with blue-leaf lotus. The silence of the night was broken by the gurgle of a fountain and the incessant croaking of a million frogs. I had heard and seen frogs before, and toads in plenty, but this bewildering cacophony of mocking frog-song unnerved me. Like the perfect cast of Kamalini's arched eyebrows, it robbed me of my confidence, so that I felt bereft and somehow inadequate.

Once again, Nearchus left me holding Arion. He walked into the house with the familiarity of someone returning home. There was an ease to his stride. For an inexplicably long time, he stayed inside, then emerged ill-tempered, looking like someone who had been thwarted in his purpose. He climbed on to his horse, and pulled me up alongside without so much as a word of explanation. We rode ahead for a considerable distance, until we came to another building, a stone and brick house with marble pillars and balustrades. I followed him, suddenly shy, for I was unsure of where I was going; the house looked too large, alien to my experience. It was full of men, Yavanas like Nearchus, with beards and without. Some were dressed in short tunics while others wore the white cotton garments of our land. There was a smell of flesh, of viands and men, not mahasamants anointed with sandalwood, but men who smelt of sweat and civet.

I could not understand what was happening around me. I heard laughter, but could not decipher where the sounds came from. We were led up a flight of steps to a suite of rooms with a carved wooden bedstead. I huddled up in the bed and fell asleep, oblivious to the noise and confusion surrounding me. Jumbled dreams swirled in my head as I slept. Just before dawn, I came awake with a cry and looked around me. I was alone. The unfamiliar room was illuminated by a patch of moonlight, broken into squares by the latticed screen on the window. I did not know where I was, and remained uncomfortably curled on the lumpy mattress, feeling a dull sense of displacement. I must eventually have fallen asleep, for I awoke, astonished, to a flood of sunlight.

With the day, I regained my bearings, and the reckless certitude of the free woman that I thought I was. From the window I saw the great sweep of the heaven-river and the majestic temples on the far shore rising into the sky. Kashi: if it did not exist, the gods would have had to invent it. I was at last in the city of my imaginings.

I was and yet I was not in the city of my imaginings. The Yavana could not legitimately live across the river, so I stayed in the foreigners' quarter on the left bank, an outcaste. I stared at the crowded ghats and gilded spires on the other shore and imagined the antiquity and true splendours of Kashi. What little I knew about it I had gathered from overheard conversations, from Guresvara, Srijan, and now Nearchus. Favoured by the deities, consecrated with a thousand temples, the kingdom of Kashi was neighboured by the jealous states of Maha Koshala and Videha. The left bank, where we were quartered, was the lesser Kashi, host to merchants and mercenaries from around the world. They came to the city to trade the fine fabrics of her looms, to buy and sell her gems and jewels, sometimes to study from her scholars and Brahmins. There were several Yavanas among them, and I learnt that not all Yavanas were from Greece, although all Greeks were Yavanas. There were also the Kala Yavanas, the dark strangers from Afrid, and the Southern Yavanas with their distinct clothes and customs.

The Kashi we lived in belonged to these foreign mlechhas, who had come for generations to Indika and made it their own. This part of the city, the Maga, did not merit pilgrimage. Those who suffered the misfortune of entering the next life from the left bank were accursed to be reborn in the body of an ass. Its local population, when ill or aged, would repair to Kashi to seek salvation. The Yavanas laughed at these superstitions, considered them ridiculous. Nearchus, too, scoffed at the blind belief in rebirth. 'The Greeks harbour ideas about the transmigration of souls,' he told me, as we looked out to the fires across the river. 'And the Christians, too, claim that their messiah, Jesus, was resurrected after he died. But Jesus was crucified, and human bodies don't decay so quickly. They may have mistakenly assumed his death. But your people—they burn the dead, roast and grill them, and think they will be reborn again! They should learn to live for the day, as I do.'

Nearchus had many commitments in Kashi; he had to collect money, pay off debts, make plans. He discussed these things with me. I listened intently, attempting to understand what I could. I learnt many things: that a hundred and twenty-four grains of gold made a denarius, that the demand for yak tails from the northern mountains was insatiable, that the Greek and Roman trade was falling, while commerce flourished in the lands of the east. But surrounded by foreigners as I was, confused by strange tongues and so many men, all this knowledge did not excite me; I felt unsettled. I preferred to stay in our room, rarely venturing out without Nearchus, and was always mildly anxious, even nervous.

Nearchus had a chest of silver coins in the room, which he kept locked. As for the coppers and cowrie shells, he would throw them around like dirt. Although he said he did not care for money, gambling aroused strange lusts in him. I became accustomed to sleeping alone until morning, when he would return, flushed and excited from a night with the dice-boards, and look at me with surprise, and sometimes with anger, as if I were an intruder or an urchin who had attached herself to him.

He kept strange company. His friends wore bracelets of gold on their arms, and glittering chains, and flaunted these baubles with the vanity of women. They would sit for hours before the chaturang board, contemplating their next move. This degree of deliberation on lifting an elephant or a pawn exasperated me. Their conversation too was unbearably crude. One of them, a thin man with dark circles under his eyes, asked me if I knew of a cure for constipation. Startled, I replied that I did not, upon which he proceeded to tell me of the effectiveness of the rind of pomegranate for the condition. On another occasion, he recommended that I resort to camel urine if ever I were vexed by body-lice. 'I am not a filthy Yavana,' I retorted, 'to be plagued by such ailments.'

Nearchus's circle of friends kept changing, for Yavanas are always travelling. I tried to appreciate their ways, but I confess it was sometimes difficult to think of those barbarians as humans. I was beginning to tire of the interminable talk about horses, although the repertoire of tricks the horse-trade resorted to continued to surprise me. It seemed common practice to drug horses with dhatura or tobacco and wine or cheap brew before a sale, to make them seem more spirited. Stable boys and grooms routinely stole their charges and sold them all over again. These exploits were discussed with hushed admiration, before the subject turned to horse races, or beast baitings, or news from the sea ports.

Nearchus had a merchant friend who was a native of Kashi. They had bought and sold horses in partnership when Nearchus had first arrived in the city. The merchant sponsored ships and caravans, and was a man of wealth and refinement. He lived in the holy city, but maintained an amusement palace across the river, not far from where we were. He invited us there for a summer festival, to celebrate the joys of the hot season.

The cruel breath of summer had been upon us through the long, exhausting ride across the plains, and I could not see what pleasure could be got from celebrating it, yet I was full of nervous anticipation. I parted my hair with a salili of porcupine quills, and attempted an elaborate plait, weaving in fresh blossoms of mogra and chameli. As I was struggling with the triple strands, the memory of the handmaiden Kamalini rose unbidden to my mind. I remembered how her deft fingers would set to work on my hair, how her cold eyes would study the subject of her labours. Another memory arose; I thought of my husband Srijan, whose existence I denied in every moment of my banishment. I lingered in these thoughts with a sweet pain that held the echoes of past pleasure, until Nearchus returned to our chamber to fetch me.

I had abandoned the braid midway, suspended half-loose below my shoulders. Nearchus commented on the style, remarking sarcastically that it hung like a horse's tail from my head. It was not a good-natured remark, there was an irritable bitterness in the way he said it. I sensed that my presence was becoming a burden on his freedom, but I was helpless, I did not know what it was that might please or displease him. I did not know that about myself, either.

A gilded carriage had been sent for us by the merchant. There were several other people already in it. I recognized some of the men, generally through the length or colour of their beards; only two of the group were clean-shaven. In all my life I had known hair to be brown, or black, then grey or white. The range of hues that Creation had lent to the Yavanas' hair never failed to startle me. Yellow, ochre, rust, and sometimes even a bright red fuzz would adorn their heads and faces, while the colours of their eyes held no less variation, ranging from amber to green to blue. I did not recognize any of the women—their faces were in any case so overlaid with paint and deceit that their own mothers would have found the task difficult. They were showy and shiny and brilliant and made me feel both resentful and superior.

We arrived at a magnificent pleasure garden. An elaborate pavilion stood at one end, decorated with streamers and toranas of tender mango leaves. The grass was freshly watered, and the summer dust had thankfully settled. Our hosts—for there were more than one, Nearchus's friend having joined with others in his guild to prepare the festivities—greeted us with garlands. Marble benches were placed among the flowers and bushes, and woven straw mats laid out for those nagariks who wished to seat themselves on the ground. Lotus-leaf fans were distributed to the guests. A panoplied stage had been set up in the pavilion, and we were informed that a play, the greatest drama ever written, was being enacted as part of the celebrations. I looked at Nearchus, surprised by this, but of course he could not have had anything to do with it. I was Yaduri to him, not the namesake of Kalidasa's heroine.

I remembered Shakuntala's story as Guresvara's tutor had told it to me, but nothing had prepared me for the actual thrill of the performance itself. The play opened with a burst of voluptuous music, employing lutes, flutes and drums, and a melodious invocation to Lord Shiva, the divine patron of all the arts. Then the sutradhar, who was also the master of events, strolled upstage and addressed the audience, as naturally as though he were part of us. His voice was loud yet perfectly controlled and modulated. It brought every word alive. The experience was both real and unreal, and I found myself submitting completely to the tale unfolding before me.

The sutradhar had curly grey hair and bore a disconcerting resemblance to my brother's tutor, resurrected from the depths of my provincial past. He called out kindly for the principal actress. Her fine, high voice trilled back. 'I'm here, good sir!' she exclaimed. 'For this learned audience, we shall now enact Kalidasa's *Abhijnana Shakuntalam*,' the sutradhar announced. 'May the actors take their parts to heart!'

The heroine, who was Shakuntala, pouted back at him. Her movements were exaggerated, yet all the more realistic for being so. 'With your able direction, nothing can be lost to the understanding,' she simpered. Her voice was like a veena.

The sutradhar turned to face his audience and struck a dramatic pose. 'To tell the truth . . .' he began, speaking in the Prakrit dialect. He paused significantly before breaking into high Sanskrit:

> I can find no performance perfect
> until the learned critics are pleased . . .
> the better educated we are,
> the more we must doubt ourselves!

I had not realized that life could be thus simultaneously observed and enacted. Intoxicated by the sure metrical flow of words, by the measured movements of the actors, I became convinced that a momentous truth or insight was about to be revealed before me. As the noble king Dushyanta and his charioteer pretended to roam the dark forests in pursuit of the antelope, I was overtaken by the excitement of the hunt. In my mind I chased the black buck with the king. While the charioteer mimed the urgent movement of the carriage, I felt I too was charging through the countryside with him. I was balanced on the very edge of my seat, and my fingernails were dug into my palms from the excitement. Nearchus was observing my reactions with considerable amusement, but I was past caring.

The scene moved to the hermitage of Sage Kanva, Shakuntala's adoptive father. The descriptions of the trees and creepers and bowers of madhavi, jasmine and mimosa took me back to my own home in the hills. I found myself nodding vigorously in agreement with the king when he pronounced:

These forest women have beauty
rarely in royal palaces seen,
The wild wood blooms outglow
the pleasure-garden creeper's sheen.

However, my namesake was a disappointment. She was far too coy and refined, constantly falling into paroxysms of shame and embarrassment. Her companions Priyamvada and Anusuya were more lively. Nearchus laughed heartily at their vulgar jokes. Shakuntala complained about her tight bark dress and asked Priyamvada to loosen it. 'Pray blame your youth for swelling your breasts—why do you blame me?' her friend replied lewdly. My lover doubled over at this, much to my distaste.

I watched wordlessly as Shakuntala abandoned herself to

Dushyanta's advances, and wondered what her father would have to say when he discovered his daughter's deceit. The play progressed. The pregnant Shakuntala had now lost the signet ring that was the memento of her secret marriage, and her lover, King Dushyanta, had forgotten the woman he had seduced in the sacred grove.

> When naïve female hearts show cunning,
> what can we expect of women who reason?

he asked her, and added:

> For the cuckoo lets other birds nurture
> its eggs and teach its chicks to fly!

I could see the men in the audience nodding their heads in sympathy. Shakuntala stood before them, shamed, abandoned, discarded, and I suffered with her the consequences of her passion.

> One should be cautious
> in forming a secret union,

declared the ascetic Sarvngarava, for:

> unless a lover's heart is clear
> affection soon turns to poison.

But Shakuntala was no ordinary mortal. Her mother Menaka was an apsara, a celestial nymph. The immortals intervened to set right the course of events and the play ended with the restoration of harmony in everybody's lives.

After the performance, elegant men discussed the sixty-four arts, and talked knowledgeably about whether Bana Bhatta was a greater playwright than Kalidasa, and *Mrichhakatikam* superior as a drama. A young dandy with red lac on his lips and a string of pearls in his hair offered me a betel leaf folded into a cone and fastened with a clove. Women attendants with bangled arms entreated us to taste a special mahasura of delicate mango wine brewed in Kashi. The wine made me nauseous, but Nearchus, of course, imbibed copious quantities of it. I sampled the unfermented sugar cane juice, which was garnished with lotus petals, and the panaka, which was flavoured with dates and grapes. I had my fill of sweet puffs and rice balls and pungent savouries such as I had never tasted before.

The actors had descended from the stage and were now seated among us. I observed them with interest. On closer examination I discovered that Shakuntala was a man, not half as beautiful as she appeared on stage, and the jester had doubled as both the charioteer and Sage Kanva. The drama was a well-constructed dream; now that I saw the impostors who had been on stage, it felt like mockery.

Later, after we returned to our chambers, Nearchus discussed the play with me, slurring his words. He was much taken with the plot, which he thought resembled the story of a certain King Pelecritus he had once heard in his own land. 'It is easy for men to forget the women they meet,' he said. 'I confess it has happened to me as well, quite a few times in my life.'

I wondered if Srijan had forgotten me. My past came back to me in an unrelenting stream. Nearchus was still discussing Kalidasa's play. 'The Yavana women in the second act . . . yes, the second act—those women who formed the king's bodyguard, they were most unconvincing!' he exclaimed. 'How can some young boy-whores of Indika do justice to the classic form of a Greek or Ionian woman?'

That night I fanned Nearchus with the lotus-leaf fan I had brought back with me, before succumbing to his ardour. But I did so with resignation, and it was not till he had reached the state of violence in his love that I responded with some passion of my own. My lover, his senses inflamed by the mango wine, spoke vile words in my ear till his fevers were stilled.

Even in the moment of her disgrace, Kalidasa's Shakuntala had the sanctity of a secret marriage. But I had betrayed everything. I had renounced my name, I was no longer Shakuntala, only Yaduri, the unmentionable one. I had abandoned the husband whose true wife I was. No matter that he had other wives before me. The noble king Dushyanta had wives aplenty, and yet there was no slur in his love-making with Shakuntala. The apsara Menaka, whose daughter Shakuntala was, had seduced the great sage Vishwamitra— but then she was an immortal, and such deeds are permitted to nymphs and celestials. Only I stood condemned.

I dreamt I was a black buck, being chased by a king and his charioteer. As the arrow struck my bleeding deer-heart, I looked into the king's eyes and saw instead my husband

Srijan, with the gold breastplate on his chest and the antelope skin wrapped around his broad shoulders. I sobbed in my sleep, and Nearchus lovingly consoled me. When I awoke to find myself in his arms I cried even more.

14

A group of chattering cleaning women came every day to the guest house in the Yavana quarter where Nearchus and I were lodged. They were low-born mlechhas of indeterminate caste. The cleaning of foreigner's dirt was outside the pale of their community duties, but it also paid better than what they would receive as wages from local households. One of these women, a tall, strong person with a faint moustache on her otherwise pleasant face, took an immediate and undue interest in my affairs. Before she set about her task of cleaning the public and private areas of the guest rooms and bath houses, she would settle down on the floor of my room, her broom of dry reeds and her swabbing cloth beside her. She would examine me expectantly, salacious curiosity writ large upon her face. Every day, without fail, she would offer me some titbit of gossip about her private life, hoping to whet my interest. She told me of her son who was sick, of her husband who had beaten her, and of a thief who had been flogged in the marketplace. She would announce the news to no one in particular, then turn to me for a reaction.

I kept my silence. I desired no confidences. Even at home, I had kept out of the way of the kitchen maids' gossip. I stayed aloof, and refrained even from asking her name.

'My name is Narangi,' she declared one day, as she gazed philosophically at the dirty pail of water before her. 'What's yours?'

'Shakuntala,' I replied. The sound of my name echoed through the room, accosting me, accusing me. 'But the Yavana, he knows me only as Yaduri.'

'Yaduri—what a name he chose!' she said reflectively. 'That's all they want, these men, if they are saints or sinners, husbands or lovers. They want to get at the raisin that lies between our legs, or return to the comfort of their mother's bosoms. Yaduri! What a name!'

She returned to my room the next morning. I avoided her gaze, but of course she was not to be deterred. 'What's in a name?' she asked, dexterously picking up the threads of our conversation. 'When I was a child, my mother had named me Rajrani! Now, do I look in the least like a queen or princess to you? Maharani of the slop buckets! I changed my name to Narangi to please myself.' She took out an earthenware jar from the folds of her clothing and left it by the latticed window screen. 'I've brought some pickled mangoes for you. My mother sent them for me from our village. I'm sure you are tired of the tasteless food these Yavanas eat.'

The sharp whiff of mustard oil and the pungent tang of

unripe mangoes filled the room. I breathed them in with deep contentment. I had heard it said that women who are with child crave sour foods. I had indeed begun to tire of the unfailing diet of rice, bread and venison on which we subsisted. Crooking my little finger into the jar, I inhaled the bouquet before licking it. It smelt of childhood and the hot summer days of my innocence.

In the evening, Nearchus recoiled from the odour as he came into the bedchamber. 'What is this accursed stink?' he demanded angrily, opening the window wide to let the smell out.

'It's pickle,' I replied, 'and it smells, as pickles do, of oil and spices.'

When we went about our pleasures he complained that I smelt of oil and spices, as street women did, but it seemed not to affect his ardour in the least. His disapproval returned in the morning, but I cared nothing for it; it was a sacrifice I would gladly make for the paradisiacal joy of the mango pickle. I ate it greedily, relishing the sharp aftertaste, bothering not at all that it had been given to me by one who was mlechha by caste. In any case I had ceded all rights to any such airs. Living as I was with a Yavana, my caste was now even lower than Narangi's.

After this when Narangi told me about herself, I had no choice but to listen. Her story wandered, as did my attention, and I took in only fragments of the confusing and impassioned tale. Her birth name, as she had told me before, was Rajrani, as ironic a royal title as my humbler, assumed 'Yaduri'. As a girl she had been married to a young man from her village, and came with him to Kashi. He left her for another woman, and another city. She had heard that he lived in Ujjaini, where he had children and grandchildren to support him. Narangi had a daughter by him, but he had taken this child with him when he left.

The intermediate part of the story was lost to me. I was not listening, only agonizing about how to ask Narangi for more of her mother's pickled mango. Whatever trials she encountered can well be imagined, but when I returned my attention to her story she was married again and mother to a young son. Her husband was a barber. He was dark and pockmarked, said Narangi, but kind, considerate and loving. He earned well and kept her in comfort. Cooking and cleaning for her husband and warming his bed, she was reconciled to her new fate and a life of adequate happiness. Narangi's husband was employed in the household of one of the great nobles of Kashi, who had his beard shorn every day in the fashion of the Yavanas. One morning, as he was shaving the noble, the barber's hand faltered and the unfailing edge of his razor slit his master's throat. Drops of blood as red as rubies fell from the blade, and the noble all but bled to his death. He survived, but the rumour spread that Narangi's husband had been paid by the noble's enemies to murder him. He lost his custom, and his good name. In his sorrow, he hanged himself from a pipala tree. He was discovered and brought down from the tree, only to succumb to his injuries. His last words were a message for his master, defending his reputation and proclaiming his innocence.

Narangi told her tale with a deep sense of drama, complete
with sounds and gestures and exaggerated emotion. I was
reminded of the play I had seen a few nights before. I was
witnessing a real-life drama, but from the inside. I told
Narangi this, but she ignored the interruption and continued
with her story. When her husband died, his scheming daughters
from a previous marriage took possession of Narangi's house
and belongings, claiming that she had been unlucky for their
father, that she was a witch who should be persecuted for
practising the black arts, and so on. The nobleman was in the
meanwhile struck by remorse. To make amends, he appointed
her husband's younger brother, who was also a barber, to his
household. Now this younger brother, Narangi's brother-in-
law, needed someone to look after his needs. He was a man,
with the natural desires of his sex, and he turned to his
distressed sister-in-law. At first Narangi shared her bed with
her brother-in-law reluctantly and grieved daily for her dead
husband. But this new lover had such skill and vigour in the
marital bed that she was soon completely infatuated by him.

'Love is a game of tug-of-war,' Narangi announced, as I
attempted to keep track of the complicated succession of
husbands. 'Only the rules are reversed. You lose the game if
you pull too hard—if you are being pulled you can be sure
you are winning it!' I tried to understand and digest her hardy
folk-wisdom, but I could make no sense of it. Narangi's new
lover, whom she still referred to as her brother-in-law, was
now ensnared by the love charms and magical potions of their
neighbour, a fat sow with bad breath. Narangi was certain he

was infatuated by her, she had seen them together, she could smell her on him. He protested his innocence, but all his earnings went to the licentious neighbour, and so it was that Narangi had to sweep and swab and clean the offal of foreigners and Yavana outcastes 'to feed her sinful stomach'.

Having resolved to abandon my pride and ask her for more mango pickle, I waited impatiently for the story to end. But this unhappy conclusion was inappropriate to such greed. I consoled her with platitudes, such as I had heard my mother speak, about how life was harsh and one must be brave. She left promising to tell me more of her life story the next day.

That night Nearchus came to me in unusual ill-humour. He did not tell me the reason for it, but expected me to submit to his rage, and I did. He slapped me violently on my buttocks, and pinched my breasts until I cried out in pain. 'I know women of your sort!' he shouted, his face set in a sneer which transformed into a snarl. 'Your sort will suck me dry of my strength and destroy me!' I was not upset by his coarse words. His anger excited me, provoked me, and I tried to further entrap him with my womanly skills. As we struggled for our joys I understood at last what the cleaning-woman had meant. Love is an inverted tug-of-war, and the one who pulls harder loses the game.

Nearchus slept, lost in dreams of distant lands and unknown women. I reflected again on Kalidasa, on Shakuntala and the ring of remembrance, pondering my own life and Narangi's story. What is a woman's desire? It is like the waxing and waning of the moon, incapable of constancy. I remembered the star of Arundhati, the symbol of fidelity to which Shakuntala's husband had tried to guide her vision. Leaning out of the window, naked, unashamed, I viewed the night sky. Raka, the moon-goddess, shone on my body. I could see no stars, only a billow of moonlit cloud illumined by the reflections of the funeral fires.

Narangi brought me pickled mangoes in the morning, but I had lost my appetite for them. She persisted with her story, denouncing the evil seductress who had ensnared her brother-in-law, but I was determined not to listen. Allowing my mind to wander away, I willed myself to recall the Sanskrit declensions I had learnt from Guresvara's tutor: 'Shakuntalam, Shakuntale, Shakuntalani.' Does the body rule the mind or the mind the body? The grammarians would say that each excites and controls the other . . .

'Your Yavana is a strong man,' Narangi said with a meaningful wink as she was leaving. 'He is built to ride women and horses.'

I thanked her profusely for the pickle. After she left, I threw it out of the window into the ornamental garden below.

Narangi did not come again to our chambers. I was relieved by her absence, and kept away from any conversational gambits from the others who came in her place.

But when the eastern breezes, the purabias, arrived, carrying the first hesitant whiff of rain cloud, I was craving sweet and sour tastes again. I longed for more mango pickles, wishing Narangi would return. She did not. One morning the new cleaning-woman came in agitated and unusually loquacious. 'You remember that Narangi?' she asked, her eyes dancing with suppressed excitement. 'Well, Narangi's dead!' she announced, without waiting for a reply. 'Her brother-in-law killed her! He slit her throat with his razor and she bled to death, poor woman. He suspected her of being in love with their neighbour!'

I left the room. I did not want to know the awful tales of women's lives, of their sorrows, their infidelities, their deaths. The pungent flavour of pickled mango rose in my mouth, before the morning sickness overcame me.

15

 'Yaduri!' he calls from the door, and before he has staggered in, I have tasted the wine on his tongue and thought of what excess will consume me, what will please him tonight . . .

Some memories cower, afraid to emerge—but the mind knows no mercy. I am in an unknown city, with a man I do not know. The dawn does not come into the day attended by the forest and the mountains here; it rises from the river amidst the death pyres. Even the river, my Ganga, is slower, there is no music in her, no laughter, as when she leaves the mountains for these flat, dull plains.

And I am different as well. This is not she who sat beside a man in an antelope skin and drank of the sacred Soma wine. Who was it that listened to the difficult wisdom of the fisherman, who sat the night through in the abandoned temple and watched the oil lamp flicker on the yoni made of stone? This is not her. This is another: she who knows no reproach, for so utter is her destruction that she is no longer there to be reproached. This is a woman without recourse.

As for this city where I witness my ruination, this is not the dwelling of the twice-born that my brother told me about in that other lifetime. It is the quarter of the Yavanas, unfinished men without a home who are to be kept away from the holy city. And so am I.

I understand few of the words that crowd around me at all hours of the day and night. These men, their fleeting, painted women—and I do not belong even among them—they speak in alien tongues. They are coarse, always shouting at each other. They laugh a lot, loudly and in a hollow manner. My brother Guresvara and I never laughed much as children, we were shy and docile. As we grew up we laughed even less, for laughter was abandon, it led to shame.

My body has abandoned itself to shame here. It hungers, lusts, contorts with pleasures that grow weaker and more desperate by the day. Darker, and more pitiful. Somewhere, the cords that connect me to my body have snapped. This could be anyone's body; I watch it with horror and a certain fascination. I am nobody; I am a body. A traveller picked me up as he might pluck a fruit from a tree, and now he is impatient to throw the core away.

There is a feast one night. A young woman who is the new wife of a Yavana soldier, a famous mercenary who has fought for many kings and many armies, has given me a dress to wear, a flowing white garment with flowers of gold thread embroidered upon it. There are also sandals to match. They are carved of wood and inlaid with gems. The dress is too long for me, so I hold it up in my hands to avoid tripping over. Besides, I want to show off the sandals. Nearchus has given me a necklace of gold and coral that makes me feel very elegant. My lips are painted a seductive red with a salve of flowers.

I am in a hall full of people. There is laughter and loud talk. Tapers light up the night as though it were day. Men and women converse with each other without shame or restraint. Nearchus is with a woman whose gown is so low that I can see the shape and curve of her breasts. It is clear that he knows her very well. I am jealous and insecure when he speaks to her.

He recites a verse to her, in the Yavana language, and the men and women in the room are all reduced to helpless laughter. He explains the joke to me.

If the parts of love-making be counted as ten,
Three thrice go to women, only one to men.

I do not find it funny. I drink a lot of wine; I have grown accustomed to the taste. It comes, I am told, from a place called Arezzo in a land called Italy, and sometimes from Persia, and also Bactria. It is brewed with grapes and fruits and is designed to send the senses astray. There is a long table. People are seated on both sides of it, men and women who are laughing and drinking and eating. Whole birds have been roasted and wrapped up in leaves, one for each of the guests. There is so much noise in the room that it makes me dizzy.

Shakuntala

A man with a pointed nose brings an oblong loaf of bread, along with a bowl of salt, and places it on the table. More wine is brought in, and a silver chalice with figures carved on it is passed around for us to share. 'This is the Loving Cup,' Nearchus explains. 'We will celebrate our friendship and love by sharing the wine.' The salt is circulated with the wine, and the guests taste it first so that their thirst grows stronger. I take a pinch of salt from the bowl, and when I sip from the cup, there is a hair on it, a golden hair from the beard of one of the Yavanas. I want to vomit, I do not want to share the Loving Cup with anyone.

Nearchus asks for a knife, but there is none. His friend, the famous mercenary, whips out a sword from his scabbard. He hands it to me. I do not know what to do and stare at it with surprise and suspicion. Nearchus holds my hand in his and guides the sword to the loaf of bread on the table. Together we slice the bread, me and Nearchus. The men and women around us clap and shout to indicate their approval. I cannot understand their language and I do not know what they are saying.

Nearchus kisses me on the lips, in full view of all his friends. He lifts me in his arms and holds me up high for everyone to see. 'You are my wife now, my delicious Yaduri!' he whispers in my ear. I am aghast. I cannot be his wife; I am the wife of another. But what can I say?

There is a man who claims he is a poet. He has a straggly beard and wears a thick line of collyrium in his eyes, as women do. He looks mad, and declaims his lines in a strange mix of many tongues. 'Life is a dance to the music of time,' he says, staring at me intently as he speaks. 'Do you comprehend what I mean?'

I do not, but I nod as though I do. He tells me of the curse of Priapus, which brings the wrath of the gods. I ask him who Priapus is. My question raises more howls and hoots of amusement. 'Nearchus, have you not introduced Yaduri to Priapus yet?' his friends mock, doubling over in merriment. I am confused. Everything I encounter is irrational. I smile to cover up my embarrassment.

The poet takes pity on me. 'The curse of Priapus brings sensuality without joy, satiety without fulfilment, degradation without grief and horror,' he says. He speaks in Sanskrit, although there are some words of Prakrit and the Yavana tongue in this grim explanation.

There is another howl of drunken laughter, and the mercenary lurches forward to give me a kiss on my lips. 'I will explain Priapus to you, my lady,' he says.

My lover is angered by this. His face is flushed, and not only with drink. 'I have married her!' he exclaims. 'Do not play with her virtue!'

'You have married her!' the mercenary exclaims in mock horror. 'And I am playing with her virtue! Why, my friend, a woman such as Yaduri can no more acquire virtue than a cook living in the kitchen can smell of roses!'

It is not anger that moves me, not hurt. I am shamed. I smile at him and quaff more wine from the Loving Cup. The carousing continues. There are squabbles and fights which nobody seems to notice. The women are flighty and talkative, like minas or brightly coloured parrots. They are behaving wantonly, for they are not women of virtue. They are like me.

I cannot breathe. I leave the room. Outside, the air is cool and clear. I am in a quiet garden, at the edge of the river, washed by the liquid silver of the moonlight. Streams of gold reflect upon the rippling water, like banners of some proud army. The fires of the dead burn brightly on the opposite bank, the holy bank. There is a sudden shower of sparks from one of them. Sounds of laughter waft out of the crowded hall. They stop in the garden, they halt, they do not dare cross the river.

The knotted arrow of the constellation Mriga is spread across the clear and blameless sky. The Sapta-rishis point towards the Dhruva-tara, the constant North Star. Nearchus calls this constellation the Great Bear. It does not look in the least like a bear to me. What am I doing here?

In the dark, I hear the tinkle of a bell. An enormous shadow stands outlined by the light of the taper at the edge of the garden. It is an elephant—I can distinguish the trunk, the four legs, and I imagine I see the white gleaming tusks, although in reality I cannot. Swaying from side to side, it has a dainty feminine walk, like the rhythm of the matagayand chhanda my brother's tutor once taught me. There is a man sitting on the elephant, the man and the elephant are as one, oblivious of the world, intent on their lonely path. They lumber into the swollen night.

My eyes fill with tears. The world is a large place. It is too large for me. I want to go home.

It is the nature of night to follow day, and day to follow night. It is the nature of water to flow. It is the nature of women to have children and grandchildren and see them grow. There is a child in my belly and I have fled from our home. What madness overcame me that day by the river? Perhaps that woman Kamalini, my dimly remembered rival, had cast a spell upon me. Perhaps it was not her doing at all, for I was born under the star of exile, like my namesake Shakuntala.

I return to the hall. Nearchus is talking to another man. 'The very fruits in this country ripen and decay faster than the fruits of any other land,' he is saying, 'and so it is with their women.'

When we met by the river, the traveller and I, when we were bodies and souls set on collision, there was innocence. There was promise.

That night, Nearchus is unsparing in his passion. My body does not respond. He takes me from behind. He is rough and brutal. I accept the pain gladly; at least it is a form of punishment.

We are still living in the foreign quarter. The true Kashi, the city of salvation, of death and destruction and rebirth, is across the river. Nearchus has promised to take me there somehow, but first there are things to sort out here. He has debts to pay off. There is money he has to collect. He is preoccupied with matters of the world, he does not have time to worry about the dreams of a wide-eyed young woman he found on a river-beach.

It is not that he is unkind. Nearchus is often tender, and we are bound together in a mysterious and indefinable way. But when he strokes my hair and kisses my lips, he has an absent look in his grey-blue eyes. He too has jettisoned something, thrown away someone who was once precious to him. At night he weeps in his dreams and takes the name Hippolytus. When, in the day, I ask him about the nightmares, he dismisses it as an old sickness, and if I persist, says only that he had a friend once, called Hippolytus, who died. I know that I cannot expect confidences, for that is not the contract between us. I hurt when he talks and laughs with other women, which he does frequently. When our bodies are not doing things together, I am restless, and my mind wanders into the past, though I resist.

One day, a holy man with two monkeys balanced on his head enters the foreigners' quarter. The sight fills me with delight. My mind returns to the black-faced langurs that clambered about in our thickly wooded hills. The holy man is also an astrologer. He reads the hands and faces of the Yavanas for a fee. He tells Nearchus that he will have many wives, and his friends, who are also listening, break into loud laughter.

The holy man notices me and stops talking in the Sanskrit-Prakrit-Yavana jumble in which he has been addressing his audience. He can see that I am not one of them. Anybody can see that. He recites a verse in Sanskrit about a calf which has wandered away from the herd, but will return to the fold and to its mother at the gloaming hour. His eyes are full of sorrow as he contemplates me.

'What are you doing here, sister?' he asks. 'Who has dishonoured you?' The monkeys on his head scratch and make faces as he speaks.

'I myself have dishonoured myself,' I reply humbly. 'This honour rests only with me.' I have not forgotten the grammarian's tricks I learnt from my brother's tutor.

One of the monkeys seated on the man's head lets out a loud screech and starts beating its chest. He takes the creature aside and whispers in its ear. They confabulate for some time before they return to me. 'The times are not good for you, sister,' he says respectfully. He speaks only in Prakrit, so the Yavanas won't understand him. 'Your stars are at variance with your true self. Have courage, and keep this talisman to wear around your neck.'

He gives me a rakshkarandak, a silver amulet in a cylindrical box suspended on a black thread. As he does, I am surprised by the voice of another that speaks from within me. 'I do not want your talisman, sir,' I hear myself say. 'I will have courage and you may leave me to my fate.'

Love is an inverted tug-of-war, and the one who pulls harder loses the game. That evening, Nearchus brings me a gift. It is a baby monkey, with a collar and a leash to keep it from running away. I can see that the monkey is missing its mother, and I grieve for its captivity. I want to let it free, but that would hurt Nearchus's feelings and I do not want to do that, either.

I spend a lot of time playing with the monkey. I try to console it, to amuse it. We make faces at each other. I regard its dexterous hands, watch it peel a banana. I observe it trying to break loose of its chain and leash. Perhaps one day I will have the courage to let it go.

As the days progress, I can feel my belly swelling up. My nipples hurt. I am often tired. Nearchus has noticed how full my belly looks, examined its roundness. I will tell him that the baby is his, it is his daughter I am carrying and she will have his golden hair, his blue eyes. He will believe me. He will never know. But I know, and regret stabs at my heart when I think of Srijan. I miss his arms at night, his broad shoulders. I put a pillow around Nearchus's back and pretend he is Srijan. He indulges me. He does not know what I am thinking, what I am going through.

Every night I watch the constellation of the thrice-knotted arrow as it sets. I examine the lights that glimmer on the river. I study the funeral pyres. As the body burns and the fire subsides, there is a moment when the skull cracks, accompanied by a loud bang that carries across the water. Once I thought I saw a figure by the pyre, an ashen woman with a garland of skulls around her naked breasts. She shone with a peculiar purple light, and stood patiently by the remains of life that the dead had left behind. These she swallowed and subsumed, more as penance than for pleasure.

16

I saw a corpse floating upon the river. Eaten by fish and river turtles, it had rotted and swollen till it looked as though it could never have been human. I enjoyed looking at this disintegrated body, it gave me a sense of satisfaction. I imagined it alive; walking, taking its pleasures. 'It is all the vanity of the senses,' I told myself, 'everything in life is only a living death.' I felt a sense of profound detachment as I articulated these thoughts, but it was a detachment my philosophical brother had warned me about. 'Shamshan vairagya, the detachment of the cremation grounds, is the easiest, most spurious form of spirituality,' he had told me, the person who had been me. 'It is, in truth, nothing but cowardice. Real detachment comes only with involvement.' I was not sure if this was merely another example of his sophisticated grammarian's wisdom, or whether it meant anything deeper. My own involvement in life had almost completely disappeared. It had defeated itself.

At last I found the courage to let the monkey go. It had grown fond of me, it was reluctant to leave. I watched it peel a banana and hold on to the skin. I saw its sad, liquid eyes regard me with confusion as I untied the corded leash around its neck. The monkey could not understand that it was free. I waved the leash in front of it but it did not make the connection. I fitted the leash back, without fastening it to the tree. The monkey would eventually realize that it was free, unbound.

The next day I found the monkey dead. A jackal or wild cat had attacked it in the night. The monkey had not run away; the illusion of the leash had been impossible to shake off. The bloodied corpse lay by the tree, teeth bared in a grimace of pain.

The time had come to leave. I knew that I loved him, but I also knew that our time together was over.

That night Nearchus could sense my desperation. He thought it was because the monkey had died. He stroked my brow and was gentle and kind. He brought me flowers from the garden, a handful of fragrant white jasmine. 'These blossoms remind me of you, Yaduri,' he said. The moonlight had crept in to illuminate the dark room. I could see him outlined against the window. His body exuded a restless strength, his eyes were alight with passion. Is it possible to burn with love and not be burnt by it? I had heard of magicians, devotees of Kali, who walked over beds of burning fire. With the blessing of the goddess, could we mortals do the same?

'I have to go to Kandahar,' he said, 'and then perhaps I will take you to Persia. The Persian beauties will appear pale and colourless before you.'

I was silent. The world is a very big place, bigger than anyone can imagine. I did not know if I wanted to see Kandahar.

'We will taste the sweetest pomegranates in Persia,' Nearchus continued, 'sweeter and redder than those Persephone ate.' I thought of the pale, sour pomegranates that grow in our hills, and the dadima tree behind my mother's house. There was a time when I would have staked anything to eat a pomegranate, to go to Kandahar, to Persia, perhaps even to Afrid, but my appetite for experience was no longer as strong. One might travel for many nights and days, but the place where one began was perhaps the only place where one belonged. My friend, the fisherman Kundan, would have understood my predicament. As I lay in that room, surrounded by sounds and smells and people I did not know, I longed above all to be at the abandoned temple, by the hidden passageway where the oil lamp flickered, where the vision of a strong and beautiful goddess had once blessed my fears.

There were tears in my eyes. Nearchus could feel them as he stroked my face. 'I have to go, Yaduri,' he whispered. 'I have no choice. I am driven by the goddess Necessity, against whom not even the fates contend!'

I loved this man. I did not know if I had the words to convince anyone else if they asked, but in my mind there was no doubt that I loved him. We shared a bond that was both tender and passionate. He recognized some part of my mind and spirit that others did not. It was not for nothing that I had left all that I knew and understood that fateful afternoon by the river. Yet I did not belong to him, I belonged to nobody, and if I was suffering my mistake I would do so scorning the pain that accompanied it.

The Yavana kissed me. I smiled in pleasure, and still my eyes were wet with tears. All of us in this world are afraid to love, it is not easy to trust and believe in others without reservation. Nearchus had loved his friend Hippolytus, and lost him. He loved me, I knew he did, and now, inevitably, he was going to lose me.

17

I awoke while it was still dark. It was the time of the first dawn. The moon had fled, but the dim half-light guided me out. I did not stumble and wake Nearchus. He slept peacefully, his hair curled about his forehead, his breath as steady as a baby's. I ached to kiss him before I left, but I did not.

A carpet of dew glittered in the garden outside. Birdsong announced the break of day. I recognized the shrill dawn songs of the harial and the kokila, I remembered them from my home in the hills. The chariots of the Ashvins had begun their journey into the sky and I could sense the warmth of the first rays of sunlight on my skin. I felt revived, redeemed. Everything seemed possible again. It was incongruous, but I was singing, a hymn to the morning-goddess. I sang it softly, for it was meant only for my daughter's ears. I was a strong woman, I was a mother. I walked across the garden to the path along the river. I was not afraid to walk alone.

I passed another elephant on the way. The mrighastin, the

beast with a hand, was plucking a branch from a neem tree. Its agile trunk held the leafy stem of young wood aloft like a flag. I stood and stared in delight, at the grey wrinkled flesh, the swishing tail, the gentle, knowing eyes. Its keeper, the mahout, stood by its side, chewing on a twig of neem. He too had wrinkled skin, and gentle eyes.

Drawing on all my courage, I went forward to stroke the mrighastin on its trunk. The keeper did not reprimand me.

'Where is it you are headed, daughter?' he asked me equably.

'I want to go across the river, to the real Kashi,' I replied. I felt safe in the company of these two, their bond seemed true and secure. 'How can I cross the river?'

'A girl of good family, and evidently far from home,' he said. It was a statement, not a question. 'What misfortune brings you here?'

'Is it only misfortune that could bring me to Kashi?' I asked in reply. 'Is it only sorrow that makes one move on from where one began? Can it not be curiosity, or the joy of travel?'

'A woman is like a cow fettered to a stump, my daughter,' he said. 'Her freedom is like the twine of duty that binds her to her household.' I was not listening. The mrighastin was lumbering down, bending its knees, sitting on the ground the way a kitten might. The mahout extracted a stem of sugar cane from his bag, which his charge instantly swallowed.

'Can I feed her?' I asked. The mahout gave me another stem of sugar cane, and I handed it to the elephant, who picked it up delicately with its long, agile trunk.

'An elephant carries its young for eighteen months,' I said, 'or so I have heard.'

'But humans, they carry their young all their lives,' the mahout replied.

I watched the elephant masticate on the leafy stems of the young neem. The river flowed before us, her waters grey-green in the light of the dawn. Already the air held the promise of a hot day.

'Soon the winds from the east will start blowing, and it will be less hot,' the elephant keeper said, reading my mind. 'And then the rains will come.'

I remembered how, when it rained in the hills, the winds lashed the trees, and the water dripped from the roof into the rooms sometimes.

'What is your name, daughter?'

'Shakuntala,' I replied.

'Get on my elephant, daughter,' he said. 'I will take you to the ferry-landing. You can go to Kashi from there.' We clambered up a folding ladder on to a large basket. I seated myself behind the keeper as the animal rose to its feet and lurched forward. There was something familiar and reassuring about its motion.

The ground was very far away. I thought of the ants that laboured in the earth, the snakes that slithered in their burrows. How distant they were. Perhaps there were animals that might make an elephant appear like an ant! What wonders the world contained! How much still remained to be seen!

The keeper held an ankush, a goad, with which he dexterously guided the mammoth beast. An elephant moves faster than a horse, I had heard, although it appears slower. Soon we were at a river wharf, where several boats were tethered. They bobbed invitingly in the water. A little girl, she could not have seen two summers, sat alone in one of them. Her eyes were smattered with kohl, and her tiny hand was dipped into the Ganga, stroking the river. There was a puddle of water in the base of the boat. If it leaked, the boat would sink, and she would drown. I climbed in to join her.

The mahout took a coin from his bag and gave it to the boatman. I wanted to thank him for this act of kindness but I did not. I sensed that travellers and wanderers in the wide world performed these acts of casual consideration for each other.

Crossing the river was exhilarating. Although there had been no breeze on land, there was a lively wind on the river. It played with my hair, rumpling it like an affectionate mother. The child was still in the boat, she sat by the prow, her hand trailing in the water as we cut across the river. I followed her example and put my hand in. How cool the water felt, how splendid! The little girl saw me and smiled.

There were two other passengers in the boat, a scruffy-looking monk and a novice wearing the white vestments of a celibate student. They were lost in animated conversation. They were discussing Mandana Misra, the jewel among scholars, who had embraced the faith of the Shankaracharya and the Vedantins.

'When the Shankaracharya visited Mandana Misra for the first time, he found even the parrots outside his house in Prayag twittering in Sanskrit!' the monk said. 'Would you believe that they were lost in philosophical discussion!—"Are the Vedas self-validated? Is action better than contemplation? Is the world real or apparent?" These were the sort of questions the learned parrots were asking each other.'

'So I have heard,' the novice replied, 'and in the most chaste and poetic language. My own Sanskrit may not have passed muster before them.' He smiled idiotically, flapping his white vestments as he spoke.

'The Shankaracharya managed to provoke Mandana Misra into a public debate, where the loser would have to convert to the other's faith,' the monk continued. 'Mandana's wife Bharati was agreed upon as the moderator of the debate.'

'A woman as a moderator?' the novice asked incredulously, his mouth open in a wide circle of astonishment. 'Am I to believe that!'

'What difference does it make?' the monk replied, quoting examples from history. 'Yajnavalkya discoursed with Gargi, and Janak too engaged with Sulabh in a lengthy argument. If such great sages could accept wisdom from a woman, why are you so hesitant?'

'There are other things I would like to learn from a woman!' the celibate brahmachari said wistfully.

'And so did the Shankaracharya!' exclaimed the monk. 'It was in matters of the Kama Shastra, and the doctrines of desire, that Bharati questioned the Shankaracharya. After all, knowledge of the body is one of the sixty-four traditional branches of learning.' The novice blushed to the roots of his shaven head. The monk tried to reassure him.

'Of course, the Shankaracharya mastered the arts of practical love only by entering the body of King Amaruka,' he said. 'I've heard that the noble king had a hundred wives. Yet the Shankaracharya managed to produce a treatise on the philosophy of sexual love in just three days and nights!'

'He always was a quick learner,' the novice joked. The two broke into uproarious laughter, which seemed to bring their discussion to a close.

There was a part of the story I did not understand. 'What happened to Mandana Misra's wife?' I asked. 'The learned Bharati, what became of her?'

'Well, the Acharya praised her for her singular wisdom and sacrifice,' the scruffy monk replied, turning to me in surprise. 'It is an honour to be defeated in debate by a great soul like the Shankaracharya.'

'Then why didn't she join the order?' I persisted. 'After all, she had argued more skilfully than her husband.'

'We Vedantins are not like the accursed Buddhist orders, where anybody and everybody can become a Bhikku, even a woman!' the monk exclaimed angrily.

Defeated, I thought of the seed in my belly. Would she blossom like the flower that smiled before me, that happy girl in the boat? I raised an inner voice, audible only to my daughter, showing her the river, talking of its ripples. In my mind's eye she could see the water, through my skin she could sense the crystal hooves of its flow. We shared the joy and adventure of our journey. 'When you are born, what will I call you?' I mused. 'Flowing with your fate, you shall be called Ganga.'

We were on the other shore. Strangely, I felt no thrill of arrival. Wide stone steps led up from the riverbank. The lower steps were cool and washed by the waves, but as I walked up, the burning stone scorched my feet. I could smell the river, its fish-and-water reek, the wet-wood odours from the boat, the unwashed stench of the boatman as he moved past me. Forlorn in the shallows, a garland kept afloat its marigolds. Between the stealthy waters of the shore and the more decided current of the river's flow, the flame of an earthen diya couraged out above the rush of water. The sight lodged itself in my heart, and it has remained there with an immediacy and urgency out of all proportion to its significance.

Through the sounds of the gongs and conches I could hear the bells; a loud, belligerent clanging such as I had never heard before. It was as though all the bells in the world were ringing together at the same time. In the hills, temple bells move as much to the will of the winds as to the touch of men and women. They are joyous and spontaneous, like the laughter of children, but these bells of the great city had something proud and arrogant about them. They were ominous, even menacing; there was no silence in between their ringing, no evasion—even the echoes sounded on. They seemed like summons to an impersonal higher presence, making me feel humble and deeply afraid.

I thought, unaccountably, of Srijan, where he must be and what he would be doing. I tried to think of Nearchus as well; he would have discovered my absence by now. Both these men seemed like shadows, I could not believe that they had existed, that my life had once been a part of theirs. Now I was alone, no one's wife or mistress, nor sister. In this frightening bazaar of people, there was only me and my unborn daughter, close and fitting, together and alone.

The bells unsettled me. Their deep and awesome clamour was forbidding. I could not climb up the steps. I lacked the courage to enter the holy city, to seek refuge. I sat down by the river and stared at the other shore that I had left behind. There was something insistent about the way the water lapped the steps, as though it was nudging me, trying to tell me something. I tried to listen, to understand what it was saying, but the crash of the waves sounded more like mocking laughter than consolation.

Well, I could not sit there forever, and in a while I started climbing up the steps. I was out of breath, and for the first time I could feel the weight of the baby I carried. Other people were appearing in the ghats now, men and women and children, more people than I had ever seen. As I walked along the upper edge of the steps I realized that the river was as full of activity as the city was. It was an extension of Kashi, or perhaps even the other way around, the city flowing around the river in varying eddies, currents and pools of stillness. Holy men with matted locks stood single-legged in the crane-mudra, offering oblations to the morning sun. Women of all ages were gathering water in brass urns. Crows and sparrows pecked at rice and grain that lay scattered as offerings. I stopped in horror as I encountered a tall, young man, completely naked from head to toe. He was taller than Nearchus or Srijan. His long hair hung loose around his shoulders, and his muscular body was smeared with ash. He was extremely fair-skinned, and the dark hair on his body stood out in sharp contrast. His penis, his lingam, protruded between his legs for the whole world to see: it stood erect and engorged, like a flagstaff or a limb of wood.

I was embarrassed, and averted my gaze, but he continued to stare at me, his coal-black eyes filled with scorn and contempt. 'You are a woman,' they seemed to say. 'Do not tempt me, do not pollute me with your wanton ways.' He tried to shame me with this look, and abruptly, without warning, some enormous, hidden, unbidden anger rose within me in response. I looked back into his burning eyes, without shame, without fear. He could not reproach me for something I had not done, for someone I was not. I considered stripping off my clothes and walking about that stone parapet as naked and unashamed as he was, with my taut breasts and my swollen belly. Why did he think he could shame me with that look? The scorn turned to anger in his eyes, then surprise, before I walked away.

I could not wander aimlessly along the stone parapet forever. Everybody in Kashi looked busy and purposeful, they seemed to know what they were doing, where they were going. I tried to look like them, as though I had a place and purpose in the workings of this great city.

In the porch of a plain, unadorned temple, shadowed by an enormous pipala tree, a Vyasa, a public reader of the sacred texts, was reciting tales from the Puranas to his audience. 'Explaining the mysteries of the Shastras is like uncovering the breasts of a mother,' he said. 'They must be well-guarded and protected, they can be revealed only to a devotee, a disciple, or an eldest son.'

I listened impatiently. It was cumbersome to sit down in my condition, but no more tiring than walking aimlessly through this busy jungle of people.

'Women and Shudras may listen to the Puranas from the mouth of a Brahmin,' the Vyasa continued, 'but they should never attempt to recite the Puranas themselves.'

He cleared his throat with a careless condescension, as though we mortals were obstructing it. Scanning the faces of his audience, he began. 'Know then that, for the born, death is certain, and for the dead, rebirth. The supreme god, Vishnu, protects the universe. By his command, Brahma creates the world; by his order, Shiva destroys it. Through Vishnu's will all beings take birth, in various wombs, human and animal, good and evil, fit and unfit. Why, you might ask yourself, would Vishnu the lord of creation enter this ceaseless ocean of birth and rebirth? Age after age he becomes a tortoise, a boar, a lion, a dwarf. Why does he abandon the pleasures of Vaikuntha, forsake his heaven to dwell in a womb, hanging head downwards, trapped in a woman's waste and urine, eating and drinking the same, tormented by worms, and scorched by the digestive fire?'

I felt the child inside me, stroked my belly to soothe her discomfort. The Vyasa continued. 'Lord Vishnu comes among us to teach us that all is Maya. All pleasure, all pain is illusion. What you gain and what you lose, what is beautiful and what is ugly—it is all the same, all is illusion. The sage Narada once went to get the blessings of Lord Vishnu. "Explain the workings of Maya to me," he said. "Teach me the nature of illusion." The lord Vishnu led the sage Narada to a pond, inviting him to bathe there. The water of the pond had been invested with the power of Maya's illusions. Narada was transformed into a female, with no memory of his former existence. The beautiful woman who had been the sage Narada was courted by Taladhvaja, the king of Kanyakubja. Saubhagyasundari, as he was now known, married the king, and was lost in the amorous life. For twelve years Saubhagyasundari took her pleasures with her royal husband. She forgot her former knowledge of the scriptures, her hard-won understanding of the world-illusion. She lived only for love, and absorbed herself in erotic activity. Then she bore Taladhvaja twelve sons and conducted herself in all the duties of a householder's life.

'At first she would worry when her sons fell ill, and fret about her husband's health. Then, as time passed, the quarrels between her sons and daughters-in-law caused her grief. When the kingdom of Kanyakubja was attacked by its enemies, and all her sons and grandsons were brutally slain before her eyes, her sorrow was great. As she surveyed the smoke from the burning pyres, her heart full of pain, the lord Vishnu came to her disguised as an aged Brahmin priest. He explained that all that had happened was bhrama, a delusion caused by the illusory play of Mahamaya. The priest led King Taladhvaja and Saubhagyasundari on a pilgrimage to the punya-tirtha. The mourning queen entered the sacred waters there and found herself transformed once again to the learned sage Narada. Great was her surprise, and her husband Taladhvaja's matched and exceeded hers! Narada realized afresh the traps of samsara, and the guile of the wanton world-goddess Mahamaya! He understood that the world is a mere dream and the true goal of all life is moksha. So refrain, good folks, from losing yourself in these deceptions. Do your duty. Fulfil your karma. Forsake the path of desire.'

My feet were numb from the uncomfortable posture, and the story had only served to depress me. The Vyasa was not done with his grim moral tales, although his audience was getting restive. I left the shade of the sighing pipala tree and hobbled out of the gathering.

A crowd of women and children were gathered around the doorway of a magnificent temple. Its spires were all gilded with gold and shone harshly halfway into the sky. I followed the crowd into the temple. A deity was being worshipped, but confused by the smells of incense, the sounds of prayer, the crush of people I could not quite understand which of the gods it was. I remembered a ritual Nearchus had sometimes followed. Before he downed the sweet red mead and became belligerent with wine-wisdom and wine-lust, he would offer a libation. 'My pious and thrifty Persian friends pour out the wine, and offer it to the unknown god,' he had explained. 'Then, of course, they proceed to drink it themselves!'

As I paid homage to the unknown one, I was pulled and pushed along with the jostle of worshippers until I found myself holding a bel leaf full of fruit and grain, a spot of vermilion smeared on my forehead. In the temple courtyard, a small group of pilgrims stood examining the carved frieze on the southern wall, which seemed to tell some sort of story. The first panel showed people dying: young women in their last throes, old men lying still before their grieving relatives, children held in the arms of inconsolable parents. The next moved to the netherworld, where the departed souls, buffeted by the waves, were trying to swim to the other shore. The pious were aided across the Vaitarani, the river of death, by Shiva's bull, whose tail they clung to with fearful desperation. Crocodiles attacked the wicked, tore their bodies apart before eating them. The horrors escalated, with the adjacent frieze devoted to the anguish of different categories of hell. A barbaric looking keeper of the dead fried evil-doers in a huge cooking-pot, turning and roasting them with a slatted spoon. Adulterers were tied to an iron rod, which was heated for their comfort.

The pilgrims, three men and an aged woman, perhaps their mother, were contemplating the panels. They seemed afraid, awed by the retributions of dharma. 'I have never stolen anything in my life,' the oldest of them said defensively. His brothers looked sceptical. I did not believe in hell, or heaven, but the sculpted visions left me queasy. I ate the prasada of fruits and grain and looked around for water. Finding no pitcher or pool, I went down again to the riverside, where I cupped my hands and drank thirstily until I had had my fill. My strength and spirits revived, I returned to explore the city.

The ramparts bordering the Ganga demarcated the Panchkosi, the borders of this noisy, happy city. It was quieter here, there were fewer people. As everywhere, the steps led to the omnipresent river, glinting in the midday sun. I had seen, heard, smelt, felt, too much. I wanted to absorb and understand it. A chariot clattered past me, from the depths of which an elegant lady with haughty eyes viewed the world with lofty indifference. An old monk in patched ochre robes walked slowly by. He was quiet, meditative. I wanted to walk with him, listen to his thoughts, but of course I could not. I was a woman, a dishonoured one at that.

'Awake! Arise. Commence a new life,' the Bhikkuni had said. I could go to a monastery, a Buddhist Sangha might show consideration for a woman like myself. Srijan's mother had been a Sakya nun. She had shaved her head and begged for alms. Perhaps I could follow her path.

18

 Three cows were clustered by the corner of a narrow, labyrinthine lane. Their warm cattle odour reminded me of home. I thought of Dasyu, and her calf. Did they miss, or even remember, me? Just this thought, and I could almost taste the clotted curds and fresh butter of the mountains. Blinded by a sudden, stinging thundercloud of tears, I strayed distractedly into the middle of the lane, and found myself directly in the path of a charging bull that appeared as though from nowhere. It raged and stamped its feet, raised its tail and flared its nostrils in a display of anger. A chanting of sacred verses rose from afar; perhaps a procession of monks. The bull bowed its head to me, as if asking forgiveness, before the city shuddered in my vision and pain flashed in my eyes like the light of a thousand suns.

There was blood everywhere: a torn womb, where my life and my daughter had been, now destroyed. As though to establish it was only doing its duty, the bull once again buried its horns in my stomach. The blood rushed out from my abdomen like a fountain, searing my face, my hands, and my feet.

The cobbled street carried on its business of life. A Kashini was tottering across the lane in absurdly high-soled sandals. This matron of Kashi held a parasol of bamboo and silk to shield her from the sun. She stumbled over me and let out a loud screech. My imploring eyes met hers; she slipped me a coin and hastily retraced her steps. My stomach heaved and contracted in unrelenting spasms as I prayed to all the gods and goddesses, for help, deliverance, anything, even death.

An apparition materialized before me, his dark skin draped in ragged strips of cloth, dry leaves on a dying tree. 'Yama, lord of death, take us from this pain,' I whispered senselessly. Hesitant, he beat the clappers in his hand. I understood. He was a chandala, the lowest of the low, who announced his arrival from a distance, for men of caste would recoil from his shadow that could pollute the high-born. Awaiting only death, I could not avoid his shadow, nor did I turn my eyes away. To this piteous soul at his feet, the chandala did not extend his cracked bowl for alms. He bent down and mumbled an apology, then made as if to touch me, but did not.

I saw the world through a thin mist. There was a stream of red running far into the cobbled lane. It shone in the sun. Beyond it, more stones, and then the river, unmoved, and beyond it, sand and forest. A dog peered at me with curiosity: a mangy, ill-fed creature from the catacombs of Kashi. Sensing my pain, it limped up and settled beside me, like an ally. A procession of holy men came into view, a company of five. The monks had tonsured scalps and shaven faces. 'Aham

Brahmasmi,' they chanted monotonously. 'Aham Brahmasmi.'
I thought I saw my brother Guresvara among them. It was he,
was it not? A luminous halo of light followed and chased him
as he walked, transparent, past me.

The monk's steps faltered only for an instant as he turned
to look. His calm eyes registered my presence. Did he
recognize his sister, who had comforted him through the
nights when he was small and assaulted by unknown terrors?
Did he now deny her, this woman fouled by blood? There
was no horror in his eyes, no disdain. There was no pity
either, nor pain. His fellow monks had not ceased their
chanting, and he walked on to join them. Men of purpose,
they marched past inauspicious sights like me. They were
god's men, in a hurry on our earth.

The mist before my eyes cleared and thickened in slow
waves. I was muttering and mumbling names from the past—
Ganga, I remember, and Dasyu. And Srijan. I closed my eyes,
but sleep would not come to me, so I opened them again. I
saw a dark muscular man, a tall man with the body of a
wrestler, ruminatively stroking his drooping moustache. I
wondered why even this strong and silent man did not come
forward to help me, until I realized that it was a vision. Yama,
the master of death, had arrived at last. With him was his
other self, his sister and consort Yami. The scene before me
was blurred with pain, but in my internal sight I could see
her, mistress and custodian of death. She was a dark figure
with radiant skin the colour of jamun fruit. Her bloodied
tongue hung from her gleaming mouth, not hungrily or

greedily, but like that of a dog tired in the midday sun. She came to me like a guardian spirit, pulling me gently by the hands from those ill-fated stones to the shelter of a deserted doorway. She stroked my brow. I clutched desperately at her cold hands, as though she were my mother, my saviour, which of course she was. She dug into my bleeding flesh, scavenging determinedly for the essence of my soul from the vehicle of my body, scooping deep into the wound in my womb. Yami took the child with her, and as she left, another figure, a human one, materialized in the doorway and smoothed her kind fingers over my forehead.

My eyes flickered from the death-visions back into this life, and I strained to distinguish the face to which the gentle human hands belonged. It was a nun in ochre robes, a Buddhist renunciate with shaven head and an impassive face that could have been carved in stone. She was kneeling down before me. Her arms cradled my head into her lap. She reached for my wrist and held it up to her ear. Suddenly I could hear it too, the ebbing away of my life force, like the rushing of a mountain stream. She listened carefully. 'I can hear the third, secret pulse, the tritika,' she murmured to a figure crouched beside her, another, dark-skinned nun in rough robes whose hands were covered in blood. 'It is the guest pulse, from which you can gauge the balance of the humours in relation to the environment. Death is visiting her guest pulse.'

They held out water for me in a small brass urn, but my mouth tasted of rust and blood and I could not drink. The water trickled out from the side of my mouth. The two women lifted me up and carried me out, through the carved wooden doorway behind which I had been sheltering. They heaved me on to something, and I found myself in a handcart with a hay mattress and the smell of incense. Together they pushed me down the street. As we progressed I saw the river stretched before me, shining and blinking in shades of silver. Earthen lamps floated on her surface, obedient to the movement of her waters, their flames put out by the waves. My thoughts, my vision, were awash with unnatural clarity. I saw the river, and below the waves I saw the fish that gorged on the flesh of human bodies, and rotting flowers, decomposing marigolds, garlands of once-fragrant blossoms.

We reached a building, and here, in a dark, quiet shed, an old woman came bustling out and applied a poultice to my wound. The poultice smelt of earth and sandalwood, and it gave me comfort. Then I was led out again, to where the handcart stood in the dappled shade of neem trees. Someone covered me with a sheet, soft and worn with use. I slept, and when I awoke the cart had been hitched to a horse wagon, and we heaved and hurtled across a rutted road. My wound still hurt but the pain had travelled, it was everywhere, in my back, in my chest, in my parched mouth which tasted of rust and salt.

Then I was in a cool hallway lined with pallets of straw and hay. It was evening, and through the pillared doorways I could hear the excited chatter of parrots, feel the faint suspicion of a breeze. At the end of the hallway was a great wall-painting of the Buddha and his associated divinities. It was lit up with the glow of butter-lamps. The Buddha's eyes, etched in gold, floated luminously before me, assuring forgiveness, promising redemption. As my eyes gradually became used to the darkness I could make out a row of nuns kneeling before the lamps. The drone of their prayers translated into words in my befuddled mind.

Buddham sharanam gachhami . . .

Retreat into the Buddha.
Retreat into the Buddha.
Retreat into the Buddha.

Kind hands fed me gruel. I ate it, grateful and content, ready equally to live or die. I dreamt of my husband Srijan. He was playing with our daughter, holding her in his arms in the grove of hibiscus bushes. In the morning my rescuer, the nun with the face which gave nothing away, dragged me outside. She examined my eyes in the sunlight, and took my pulse again, and seemed dissatisfied. The poultice which had been applied to my stomach had dried up and contracted, and a dull throbbing pain lay alive beneath it.

The sky was sometimes grey, sometimes blue, like the colour of Nearchus's eyes. A black kite fluttered far among the clouds. Perhaps it was once again the month of Magh, the month in which I had been married. A striped squirrel came up and examined me with cautious eyes. A mina burrowed in the mud for grains. A large lustrous crow hopped over and perched itself by my head. It was time for me to die.

19

To face death is not as difficult as one might imagine. The main point is that there is very little time. Everything happens in such a rush, so suddenly, that there is no place for terror. Time contracts even as it expands. It becomes irrelevant, as does everything else. There is, at the last frontier, no pain—for the body has its own defence against extreme pain—only a luxurious sense of surrender, of giving up responsibility. And yet I held out.

All around me I could hear the soothing hum of prayer wheels and the solemn chants of 'Om Mani Padme Hum'. Sanity lay in dying, in yielding to my fate. But as I heard the crow caw by my head and watched the dark Sankranti kite blur in a haze, I knew that I could not surrender yet. I had to return home, to Srijan. It was not him that I had run away from. I had set out in search of a part of myself, and it had eluded me. I had not traded one life for another.

The dispassionate face of the nun appeared before my failing eyes, looming unnaturally large. It was not a serene face, though she was kind; it was controlled, the muscles held in, the mind sternly steadfast. I wondered if I could tell her of my wish. But what was the way back home, in which direction? And when I tried to speak, I could not, for by then I had no voice left. The nun put a pad of moist cloth on my mouth to soothe my dry lips. 'Sister, accept the Buddha before you die,' she whispered. 'Renounce the world and yield to him!'

Black clouds had gathered above us. I heard the din of distant thunder, and a streak of lightning rent the sky. Hot drops of rain fell on my face. I smelt the gratitude of the damp soil. They carried me in again, to the lightless hallway, and lowered me on to the pallet. Expertly, the nun rearranged the contours of my limp body. Her face was in shadow. She sat by me through the night, this nun whose name I never came to know. She spoke to me softly, in an urgent whisper that sounded like a wheeze, as though she were just a little breathless. 'Listen to me, little sister,' she said. 'The world has abandoned you, and perhaps it is now time for you to abandon it. Fate has brought you to the sanctuary of the Deer Park, the most blessed spot on the face of the earth. There is a pattern to fate's tricks. Why else have you been brought here but for your redemption? The Buddha has picked you up for your salvation as a crow might pick up a piece of bread!'

I found the simile strange, but I was too tired to protest. 'You are at the monastery of the Deer Park,' she continued. 'When you are better we will walk together in the gardens, through the grove of penitence. There is a wall around them which keeps us safe from the evil world outside. We will wander together among the balustrades and the two-storey palaces, and I will show you the Vihara, the temple monastery. I am sure you will never have seen such splendour before. It is made almost entirely of gold, although the foundations and stairs are of course of stone. Surrounding the Vihara are a hundred rows of niches, each containing a statue of the Buddha, embossed in gold. When you enter the Vihara you will see a statue of the Sakyamuni, larger than life! It is cast in bronze, but when you see it I know you will imagine that it breathes!

'When you get well, little sister, we will walk around the Vihara. To the west is a sacred tank, where the Sakyamuni used to bathe. A little to the west of that there is another, in which he washed his monk's water-pot; and a short distance to the north, there is a third, in which he washed his garments. The waters of these sacred tanks will surely cure you of your ailments.'

I wandered in and out of sleep even as she talked. I dreamt of the old temple, and the secret passage. I thought I saw the eyes of the filthy crone who had once accosted me there, but no, it was the nun again, still telling me about the monastery of the Deer Park. 'There is a statue of the Tathagatha,' she wheezed, 'it is set in the centre of the garden, on a pedestal, as though he were walking there above us.'

I tried to open my eyes. I could see her sitting beside me in the dark hall. The implacable eyes of the Buddha, painted on the wall, lit by butter-lamps, confronted me. I tried to evade their calm stare. My breath was getting shorter, I could not breathe, it felt as though pebbles were rolling inside my chest. The nun turned to her assistant, who was sitting silently beside her. 'Observe the breath,' she whispered. 'Such long shallow gasps are called the dog's breath. They indicate that the end is near.' She took my head in her arms, as she had done when she knelt beside me in the doorway. 'Embrace the Buddha,' she said. 'It is the only way.'

Something of my old stubborn spirit rallied around even at that moment. I was offended by her tone. I would not be bullied. I would not embrace the Buddha only to please her. Summoning all my waning strength, I turned my face slowly away from her reproachful eyes. I was breathing with great difficulty. The nun and her acolyte placed a square slab of stone on my chest to ease the breath away.

I saw her again, the death-goddess, her tongue the colour of blood, who sought me out with such persistence. Eluding the soul-snatching nun, I leapt into her arms.

Feeding on memory, feasting on the refuse of hopes and dreams, her breasts covered only by a necklace of grinning skulls, she may appear cruel, but Kali is in fact a gentle goddess. There is no pain in her realm, as there is no hope. But she could not console me; I would not let her. She would have me, but not before I had travelled upriver, as the mahseer fish do, to spawn in the monsoon streams of their first memories. I did not seek release; it was just that I could not forget.

The laws of karma play themselves out at three levels: in the ether of our thoughts, in the consequences of our actions, in the finality of our fate. Of these triple strands of destiny, in only one was it ordained that I would ever go back home. As a flame is extinguished so I had died in Kashi, which was a blessing. But I did not will it so. The bile, the defeat, the ignominy in this death—I rejected it. I would not depart humiliated from these shores. I would hide, escape, return to the earth and the rocks that knew me, and the parrots, and the patient fisherman who sat by the banks of the Ganga, baiting her fish.

I had no body to slow me down, my feet were not weighted with silver anklets, my breath did not chase itself in and out of my chest. But I learnt very quickly to be cautious, for the Ganga swarms at all times with guileful souls fleeing to and from their destinies through her waters. On the way, I saw a jackal, scavenging on decaying bodies of humans and animals. Like me, he was a soul in escape, a refugee from what must be. He lurked by the river's edge, this creature with sly eyes and a subtle grin. Glimpsing my shining shadow-self he ran after me in pursuit, attempting to lure me into his furry coat and take over the burden of his karmas. Dissembling by the water's edge, he tried every trick and ploy in his animal cunning, but I continued my journey, intent on my destination.

A soul in flight is a dazzling sight, it shines and gleams and glitters for those who can see it. The furies who accompany the lord of death sighted my soul fleeing like a flapping, radiant butterfly, and hunted after it. But the lady of the burning ghats, the devourer of desires, habituated to greed and fear and grasping, to craven pleading, was moved by the courage of my battling soul, and granted it safe passage.

It travelled upriver past the groves and glades where Nearchus and I had made love to each other, past the rocks where we had sat and rested, the horse tethered beside us. Then, near Gangadwar, where the river leaves the mountains and descends to the world of mortals, my shadow-self came upon the rock where I had offered oblations of milk for the safety of my unborn child. At this spot my resolution faltered. Was it here that I had failed in my duty? As my resolution faltered, so my strength diminished.

Ganga, granter of immortality.

20

After Shakuntala had first disappeared by the sacred rock downriver, Srijan was distraught with grief and anxiety. He sent out search parties in all directions, timid village men who combed the forests as best as they could. He alerted merchants who travelled the trade routes, asked wandering mendicants to help, sought auguries from the entrails of slaughtered chickens, but he received no news of his wife, his beloved Shakuntala. Then a body was found on the left bank of the river, a corpse devoured by jackals, rotted and decomposed beyond recognition. Some things about it suggested it may have belonged to a young woman. So it was cremated with all ceremony by the riverbank. The village priest officiated at the funeral, and privately shed tears for the beautiful, errant girl who had been Srijan's wife.

Srijan wept and grieved and longed for his lost wife as he had done for none of the others who had preceded her. He was duly consoled by Kamalini, of the haughty demeanour.

The handmaiden blamed herself entirely for what had happened, admitted she had been derelict in her duty to her mistress. She did all she could to comfort Srijan, and in time became his wife. Srijan did not allow her to touch Shakuntala's clothes and jewellery. He kept these in her wooden dower box, which he opened occasionally when he thought of her, the bird that had flown away.

But he was a practical man, and the bedchamber he shared with Kamalini was the same as the one he had shared with all the wives who had come before.

00

 Three cows cluster by the corner of a narrow lane. Their warm cattle odour reminds Shakuntala of home. She can almost taste the clotted curds and fresh butter of the mountains.

A chanting of sacred verses rises from afar as a procession of monks comes into view. The tallest of them has the look of Guresvara about him: the same hesitant kindness, the imperfect aloofness. Is it really he? They are still too far away. She is not sure if she should move towards the monks, or hide. From somewhere behind them, a bull breaks belligerent, scattering their numbers, silencing their prayers. With single-minded intent it charges towards Shakuntala. Her womb is split open like a pomegranate, blood-pearls scattering on the cobbled street.

A monk rushes towards her. With a swift movement of his saffron vastram he whips the angered animal. Shiva's bull accedes to this chastisement and rambles away. The three cows, immutable as the triple strands of fate, continue to ruminate on the remains of temple offerings and prasada.

Tottering across the lane in absurdly high-soled sandals, a matron of Kashi, her skin the colour of the jamun fruit, crosses Shakuntala's line of vision. She is shielded from the sun by a bamboo and silk parasol. Shakuntala's imploring eyes meet hers. 'My daughter must live,' they plead, voicelessly drawing the Kashini. The lady minces across the bloodied cobblestones to kneel by Shakuntala's side. Her face is impassive, but not unkind. Careful fingers gouge Shakuntala's womb, feeling about the gore for signs of life.

'Give me your vastram,' the Kashini says to the monk in a voice of command. Humbly, he hands her the ochre garment that had kept the bull of Shiva at bay. She winds the cloth around the dying woman's stomach. Instantly the vastram takes on the deep, rich sheen of spilt rubies.

Shakuntala is overcome by pain. She heaves and writhes in agony. The jewelled rings on the Kashini's fingers lacerate her wounds as she manipulates the labour. There is a wail of life, a soft, sure cry like a whelp.

'He lives,' the monk says, in a voice saturated with awe. 'By the grace of Shiva, he lives!' He extends his arms to claim the boy.

'There is another one!' the matron exclaims. 'Another life in her womb!' Shakuntala hopes, waits, for her daughter. The monks' chanting grows distant, with the receding sounds of a child's cry. 'The men of god have taken your son with them,' the Kashini says. 'You are fortunate that he is in their care.'

Her lips draw blood as she pulls and strains to force the

residual weight from her body. The Kashini comforts her, strokes her damp forehead. Shakuntala smiles as she dreams of her daughter, the life they will share together, alone. Her mind wanders, and she is in the womb of the abandoned temple, in the garbhagriha where the oil lamps flicker and the yoni is strewn with blossoms.

She can feel the Kashini's jewelled fingers easing the child out. She waits patiently for the howl of pain that announces arrival, but she hears nothing. Time expands and contracts.

Shiva, Smarahara, the destroyer of memory. He bends over her, whispering his Taraka mantra in her ear. She sees the maddened eyes of his mount, the bull, whose horn now glistens above her like the crescent moon on his Master's brow. Death-visions surround her. Is it the river she hears, or Shiva's damru, the beat of time, drumming in her blood, forcing her breath away? She strains to hold on to her daughter as the Kashini restrains her: 'The world has no place for us,' she whispers.

With the sun at half-low, the afternoon stood still. A white light glared down at me. Kind hands held out water in a brass urn, but my mouth tasted of rust and blood and I could not drink. The river roiled and swelled with unease. A gust of anger rose inside me, compounded of contempt and clarity, and of exhilaration. It did not matter, I realized, that I had lived my life one way rather than another. The world would always have its way; at least I had searched for mine. That was the Taraka, Shiva's mantra of deliverance.

Perhaps I slept, because when I awoke the stars were shining on my face. I could see the familiar constellation of the thrice-knotted arrow. The girdle of Orion, Nearchus had called it. When the Dog Star rises, he had said, the lands around the river Aigyptos are consumed by floods. The world is a very large place, but here, by the river, the gentle night breeze cooled my temples, and the sound of the waves was like a caress.

The Ushas had spread the web of the false dawn across the sky. It was the Brahma-mahurta, when the Creator holds all the worlds in balance. I glimpsed the years that might have come, they were like the breath of the morning, a whisper in my ears, an invitation. Then the temple bells sounded in an unceasing clamour.

After a long time I thought again of my mother, how she had never been afraid of anything. I remembered her face, anxious and alert, as I clambered up the cliff face in search of silajita. Were there tears in her eyes?

'Don't weep for me,' I murmured, to nobody really. I would not weep for my daughter, I would not waste my tears. I had not wasted my life. I had lived.

Like a minor wind, I saw myself afloat and rising.